HIRED DATE ON THE ISLANDS

The Island Series Book 2

By Dove Devereaux

HIRED DATE ON THE ISLANDS

By Dove Devereaux

First edition published April 2022
ISBN No: 978-1-9168722-3-3
Paperback Edition

For enquiries, contact the publisher at dovedevereaux.com

CHAPTER 1

'I spoke to your brother last night and it got me thinking.'

CJ Connors rolled her eyes. She'd known her mum was up to something when she rang at the last minute to suggest they met for lunch. All through their meal she'd chatted about everyday things but now, right as they were about to leave, she was bringing up the real reason behind it.

Her mum had just handed her bank card to the waiter, brushing away offers to contribute to the bill.

'Is it that late?' CJ started to ease herself up from her chair. 'I've got an appointment so am going to have to dash, sorry. You can tell me what it was on the phone later.'

A panicked look crossed her mother's face. 'You're going already? But I wanted to talk to you about something important.'

CJ slumped back into her seat. 'Don't worry, I'm kidding. Come on, out with it – what's so important?'

Her mum aimed a playful swipe at her. 'I should've known you were winding me up. Anyway. I don't know if you've spoken to Tim since he got back, but he and Charlotte obviously had a great time on their holiday.'

'He sent me a few photos. It looked idyllic.'

CJ remembered some of the beach photos her brother and his girlfriend had sent her

from Tenerife. She'd could still feel the pang of envy she'd felt looking at the sun-drenched snaps, while the rain had beat against her office window.

'I think you should have some time away too.' Her mum searched her face. 'You've been looking so pale lately, I'm worried about you.'

'Mum, I always look pale and so do you. That's what happens when you have our colouring.'

CJ and her mum both shared the pale skin, red hair and striking green eyes of their Irish ancestors. Nowadays her mum's hair was streaked with grey – a natural look which most people wrongly assumed was the result of spending a small fortune at an expensive hair salon.

'You know exactly what I mean, CJ. You've got less colour in your cheeks than usual. It's been a tough few months but now we're out the other side, you need to follow in your brother's footsteps and have a break.'

A tough few months was an understatement. CJ's beloved grandfather had fallen down the stairs, badly injuring himself. Fortunately, he was discovered quickly, but because of his age it had been touch and go for a while. She could still feel the wave of relief when the doctor finally confirmed that he'd be OK. But the family's joy was short lived; he'd picked up a chest infection, which turned swiftly to pneumonia. His condition became critical, with medical staff advising them to prepare for the worst. It had been the most terrible time of CJ's life and even now she could feel tears forming as she thought of it.

She blinked them away quickly before her mum could see. 'It's a nice idea but I don't have time at the moment.'

'And that makes me feel awful.'

'Why?'

'I feel bad that you and your brother took time off to help out when Grandpa was poorly and now you're worn out, with no chance of having a break. You don't want to make yourself ill.'

CJ pulled her chair in a little further to let a couple pass. 'I'm fine, honestly. Don't worry.' She reached out and patted her mum's hand. 'I can't go at the moment because I'm really busy with the business. Besides, Tim can head off with Charlotte. I have to wait until one of my friends is free, or go on my own.'

'There's nothing wrong with that nowadays, as long as you're careful. Lots of people holiday on their own. Next time you go away for business, why not tag a few days on the end?'

'You're not going to let this drop, are you?' CJ laughed as the waiter returned.

Her mother thanked him, took back her bank card and put it in her purse. 'No CJ, I'm not going to let it drop. What's more, Grandpa agrees with me.'

CJ threw her hands up in the air. 'Whoa – now you know that's not fair.'

She'd do anything for Grandpa, especially since his recent illness. It used to be the other way round, when she was small CJ could wrap him round her little finger. He'd taken on the day-to-day role of father figure after her parents split up and her dad moved away for work. But as CJ got older, the dynamic changed and now Grandpa could wrap her around his finger instead.

Her mother shrugged. 'He was concerned too. I'm only relaying it.'

'But you know I won't want him to worry.' She dropped some coins onto the table for a tip.

Her mum started to put her purse into her bag, before pausing to look at her daughter. 'Tell you what, suppose I tell Grandpa that the next time an opportunity to take a few days away comes along, you'll take it? How would that be?'

CJ rose to leave, laughing and shaking her head all at once. 'That would be blackmail, that's what that would be. OK, I give up. But you can tell him from me it's unfair that you've both ganged up on me.'

Her mum opened her arms and CJ stepped forward for a long hug, breathing in the familiar, comforting perfume that made her feel like a little girl again. She and her mum were both spirited and during CJ's teenage years that had led to some difficult moments, but now they were as close as could be. Even more so since the recent family troubles.

'I'm off to see Grandpa now, so I'll tell him we had this chat. Can I say you promise to go away the next chance you have?'

'OK Mum. I promise.'

As they linked arms and strolled happily down the street, CJ thought how lucky she was. She sent a little 'thank you' to the heavens, happy that her troubles were all behind her.

CHAPTER 2

'Lap 60.'

Jake Masterson touched the tiled wall with his fingertips and surfaced from the pool. He pulled off his mirrored goggles, wiped the water from his face and shook his blond hair.

His breathing was heavy from the strenuous swim he'd put himself through but to his annoyance he realised it hadn't worked.

'Damn it!'

He tossed his goggles away and they drifted gently towards the bottom of the pool. Jake put his hand out before they went too deep, scooped them out and put them onto the side, then rested his shoulders against it and leant back.

It was unusual for him to swim at lunchtime. He usually worked out early in the morning – as he had already today – but he'd spent so long staring at the offending page on his screen that eventually he'd snapped the laptop shut and dialled up his executive assistant, who was in the London office.

'Paul, I'm going down to the pool house for a swim, so I won't be contactable for a while.'

If Paul had thought it unusual that his boss was taking a dip in the middle of the day he'd not said so, but merely promised to take any messages to pass on later. Jake was relieved he'd chosen this day to work from home. He tried to do at least a couple a week nowadays; he liked the ability to enjoy his lovely home and grounds but also to finish work earlier than when he commuted up to town. It wasn't only for his own pleasure, he had responsibility for Xanthe now too. The precise days varied from week to week, depending on his other commitments, so it was pure chance that he could make use of his sports facilities today.

He'd hoped – no, assumed – that some hard and fast lengths of his pool would clear his mind; it had always worked before. This time, however, the answer he sought evaded him. He contemplated putting his goggles back on and swimming some more, but doubted it would work.

Cursing, he pulled himself easily onto the side, the water running down his muscular chest and legs, before pooling at his feet. He'd had to work-out hard every day for many years – first for his modelling career and then for the physically demanding roles of a movie star. Keeping fit was the less glamorous part of the job. Now he was a full-time businessman and only took on a few film roles, so had less need to exercise as hard. But he liked the way his workouts gave his body – and particularly his mind – real strength.

Wrapping a soft white towel around his waist, Jake padded across to the changing room. He spotted the clock on the wall and it transported him back to the reason he'd been so frustrated in the first place – seeing the looming dates on his calendar.

He made a face. It was so ridiculous, to get wound up about something so minor. After all, there's no shame in going on a business trip alone…again.

Until recently he'd welcomed the solitude, which served as a barrier to the outside world. But seeing lots of friends settling down had triggered something, and Jake had started to wonder if a life alone was truly what he wanted. As a result, he'd started to take some tentative steps into the outside world again and had confidently assured his business associates — who were now friends — that he'd be bringing someone along.

'Not that I care about going on my own, or what other people think,' he muttered, throwing on his T-shirt, which clung to the dampness of his body.

Jake was now in the enviable position of working because it interested him and not because he needed the money. Even if he stopped work today, he would never be able to get through all of his fortune in his lifetime.

So why was it this occasion had got under his skin? He stopped for a moment and thought, staring — without seeing — at the stunning view of the west gardens beyond. He delved in his mind for the reason until he found it and brought it into view to examine.

Now it made sense. He'd seen the forthcoming trip away as something of a marker in the sand. When the invitations had been issued and arrangements made, some six months or more ago, he'd felt confident he'd be in the throes of a serious relationship by now. Surely it would be as easy as last time, falling into something before you even realised it, getting serious without ever needing to think things through…letting everything happen naturally…

And yet.

Jake might be older and wiser, but nowadays he assumed everything would go his way and it was a shock when it didn't. This assumption wasn't arrogance or dumb luck – sure, he'd had some chances along the way, but he'd utilised every one. No, things went his way because he was a hard worker and a straight player. There was only one thing that had gone badly wrong in his life to date, though that had coloured and shaped him forever. Since then, he'd worked even harder, as if to prove to himself he wouldn't fail at something again. That was why it annoyed him so much that a relationship had eluded him, even though he wasn't totally sure he even wanted one. What a mess.

He grinned as he heard his mother's voice in his head: 'Have you considered talking to someone? A professional I mean. A therapist would love to spend some time with you.'

She didn't know the half of it and if she did, she'd probably drive him to a clinic herself.

He finished dressing, then headed back to the lift, to his home office. The swim had merely acted as a temporary distraction. He needed to approach the forthcoming engagements as he did anything else, figure out the issue and then find a solution. His first question, was he happy to go solo, or not?

'And if you're not happy to go alone, Jake Masterson, then you've got to work out how to fix it.'

Speaking to the dating agency he'd joined was the obvious first move. Paul had made all the arrangements with them so far. Maybe the personal touch would bring about more success?

With a fresh coffee in hand, Jake logged back onto his laptop. It shouldn't take long to call and discuss whether there was someone new who might be willing to accompany him for some of his trip. The women he had met so far were incredible but he'd shied away from any attempt to take things further, so didn't want to ask any of them to accompany him. The last thing he would do was lead someone to believe a relationship was developing when it wasn't. He'd ruled out taking his mother because she needed to be there for his dad. Xanthe was too young, and his sister had a young baby. Mentally, he ran through the faces of his female friends but none would be available. He'd just have to find someone and make it clear it was purely a business arrangement. Before he could change his mind, he started to search for Hearts & Mind Dating.

It was first in the list of results. Hardly surprising. A couple of years ago an up-and-coming actor had found his life partner through the agency and had told everyone about it when promoting his film. It had propelled Hearts & Mind Dating to the top of the industry.

Jake clicked on the link and went straight to the About Us section. His breath caught in his throat.

Perhaps it was a particularly good photo, but he'd not expected the head of the agency, CJ Connors, to be such a stunner. To be honest, he hadn't given her looks any thought at all and if he had done, would've imagined someone a lot older. Yet the photo on the website was of woman in her early 30s, at a guess. He was struck first of all by her hair – shoulder length and smartly layered and a deep russet colour, which shone from the page. Jake wondered what it felt like to touch.

CJ Connors was smiling into the lens, her green eyes shining in the light. They danced and twinkled and, coupled with her wide smile and a smattering of freckles, her whole face glowed. He'd seen lots of publicity shots in his time, but few where the whole personality was captured for all to see. Positivity and happiness shone from his laptop screen and unusually he realised he was smiling too.

'Wow!'

Then an idea formed. An idea which was crazy and audacious and very unlike him. Jake scrolled across to the Contact Us section, before he could change his mind.

If CJ Connors thought the phone call she was currently taking was tricky, it was nothing compared to what was coming.

CHAPTER 3

'We had lots of the same interests and it seemed to be going brilliantly. There was a spark too. At least I thought there was. What do you think went wrong?'

CJ frowned. 'I'm sure nothing went wrong, it's probably just a misunderstanding,' she reassured her client, even though inwardly her heart sank. She was standing by her desk, phone clamped to her ear. Lunch seemed a million years ago.

'Don't worry. I'll look into it and come back to you.'

An hour earlier her day had seemed so different. Fresh from meeting her mum, she'd started working through the outstanding mail, tearing open a thick, cream envelope to reveal a wedding invitation from James and Lucy, whom she'd first matched two years ago. With a big smile she'd placed it into the in-tray, alongside some less welcome invoices. There'd also been a postcard from Jane and Will, who were on their first holiday together on a beautiful Caribbean island. The card showed a sun-kissed beach, and CJ cast her mind back to the promise she'd made her mother and grandpa. Little did they know it was an easy promise to make, given CJ had got no business trips booked.

Even so, a few days away would be welcome.

There was more good news in her emails – David and Mark's second date had gone really well and they'd fixed to meet up again. Steve and Philippa were looking at houses together. How she loved her job!

That was until she read the message from Sally, asking her to call. So here CJ was, listening to yet another tale about the disaster that was Jake Masterson.

'He's extremely charming and attentive. And talk about good looking…' Sally gave a low whistle. 'Have you ever met him?'

'Not personally.'

Therein lay the problem. CJ tried to insist on meeting all Hearts & Mind Dating clients because that was her best guarantee of success, but in this instance she'd been given a firm 'no'.

'He's so much more handsome than he looks in his photos and films, and he looks damn good in those.'

CJ wasn't surprised. Former model, turned film star and now entrepreneur Jake Masterson looked stunning in everything she'd ever seen him in. His office had sent photos over when he'd joined her agency and she glanced at those now, his blond hair cropped short, the smart linen suit barely disguising the impressive physique beneath the fabric. His square jaw was strong, but it was his eyes which captivated her. They were a rich hazel-brown, like a fire-lit, autumnal evening and they sparked off the page.

'Very handsome,' CJ murmured dreamily, forgetting she was still on the call.

'I'm sorry, what?'

'Oh…err…nothing, Sally, nothing. You were saying?'

'I was saying we had a fantastic time but when I invited him round to mine for coffee, he declined.'

Maybe he prefers tea? CJ smiled at her own joke as she took a sip of the warm liquid from her cup. Sally was a highly intelligent, dazzling woman, so whether it was merely coffee she was offering – or more – it showed some character on Jake's part to decline. He went up in CJ's estimation, though she was still concerned that he seemed to be playing some sort of game.

Sally was still relaying the tale. 'Not only did he say no, even though there were no strings attached, but he also said that while he'd had a great evening, he didn't think it was a good idea if we saw each other again. What do you think of that?'

CJ was no longer surprised. Sally was a perfect fit – accomplished and bright, yet she was the latest in the long line of Jake Masterson rejects and quite frankly, CJ thought that finding him a life partner was her most challenging task to date.

She made reassuring noises about following it up, before ending the call. In her silent office she picked up the photo again and looked at it more closely. His face was impassive, the slightest hint of a smile making him seem neither cold, nor particularly friendly – a bit like the male equivalent of da Vinci's Mona Lisa.

'Who is the right person for you?' she asked the picture. 'And why do you dismiss people so quickly? Can't you give them a chance, get to know them?'

In the six years since she had established Hearts & Mind Dating, CJ had never come across such a difficult customer. She prided herself on the method she'd painstakingly developed to find the perfect match for her clients, which had brought about considerable success. Using her psychology expertise, she'd developed her own specific formula for matching couples together. To date it had given her one positive result after another and coupled with her complete discretion, her reputation had soared. Now she was sought after by the rich and famous. Yet Jake Masterson, had met a succession of truly fabulous women – lawyers, entrepreneurial single mums, doctors and politely rejected each one after the first date. CJ's brow wrinkled. What is it with him? If he's not ready for the dating scene, why approach the agency?

She slapped his folder onto her desk. This wasn't just potentially damaging to the business, but the women on her books were fantastic. With little time to socialise, they'd come to her for help to find someone special. Yet here was Jake Masterson, turning them all down, one by one. Maybe she should turn him down.

CJ busied herself with looking up the star's contact details. Meeting the clients face-to-face gave the best chance of success. He'd been busy launching a new company a few months ago but perhaps she should try his office again, see if he now had the time? The questionnaire had given her some information but the way it was worded made her suspect that someone on his team had filled it out. If she could meet the man, she might have a shot.

She was flicking through her files when the phone rang and she snatched it up automatically.

'Hearts & Mind Dating.'

'Sounds interesting. Miss Connors? Jake Masterson.'

CJ almost dropped the phone in shock. She knew that voice immediately from his many films. Were his ears burning? Did he have some sort of psychic ability, so knew he was being thought of?

'Wwwhhat can I do for you, Mr Masterson?' She was cross for being thrown and tried to get herself together. Answering the phone to someone famous wasn't new to her anymore and no doubt Jake Masterson was calling for the same reason Sally had – to discuss progress and what to do next. She swallowed hard and tried to concentrate.

'It's simple.' He spoke with business-like efficiency. 'I need someone to accompany me next week on a very important business trip. There will be several important clients there, all bringing partners with them. Obviously, given your reputation, I'd thought I would've met someone to take with me by now, but unfortunately that's failed to happen.'

CJ bristled. It wasn't her fault he was so difficult. She decided not to comment and instead let him continue, before almost falling off her chair at his next words:

'As you've failed so far in your attempts to find me someone suitable, then I can see only one solution to this issue. It'll have to be you, Miss Connors. You will be my date next week.'

CHAPTER 4

Jake waited patiently for CJ to reply. He realised his statement would likely floor her – why, the idea had even surprised him. It was bound to take her a few seconds to get her head around what he'd just said.

'Mr Masterson, I arrange dates, I'm not the date,' she said finally.

'I realise that, but given all of the women you've sent so far have been totally unsuitable and I need someone to accompany me to a crucial business event, you'll have to do.'

'Have to do?!'

He could hear her splutter on the other end of the phone.

She must wonder what era he was living in. It was hardly the 1950s and he could go to the event on his own. He was used to it and in the early days, with grief raging through his very core, hadn't wanted anyone else there with him.

'It would be highly unprofessional for me to accompany you and besides, I don't have the capacity to be away from the office at the moment.' CJ appeared to have got over her initial shock and was now speaking in professional, clipped tones. 'You may not realise this but I run my business on my own and it's incredibly busy.'

Jake raised his eyebrows. He'd imagined she had a whole team of people working for her. That she'd achieved all this on her own was impressive, though it didn't change the matter in hand.

'Isn't that part of the package I've already paid for – for you to get to know me personally so you can find the right date? So, I'd have thought this trip is necessary, given your track record so far.'

His provocation was met by a loud snort.

'And don't worry, I'll make it well worth your while. An offer you can't refuse. It seems like the perfect solution for both of us.'

Jake's idea may have been left of field but as he'd placed the call, he'd quickly worked through one or two arguments that she might come up with for not attending. Fortunately, he wasn't someone with a huge ego who assumed everyone would immediately be flattered that he'd even asked. Indeed, it was something of a relief that CJ Connors was putting up such resistance.

'But as a favour to you I am prepared to pay for your additional time. I think you'll find my terms are very generous,' he added.

'A favour to me?'

He could tell she was still reeling but he wasn't going to let up, not this close to succeeding. He chose not to reply, leaving her with a silence to fill.

'And I'm not interested in the money,' she said, eventually.

'No?'

'Absolutely not.'

'OK, well I guess there's one thing for it. We'll have to agree to part company. I'll no longer be a client of Hearts & Mind Dating.'

CHAPTER 5

It wasn't an idle threat. Jake had already decided that if CJ wouldn't accompany him on his business trip to the Isles of Scilly, there was little point in continuing their business relationship.

'I can't see any other way forward,' he ventured. 'It's a shame your company hasn't kept its side of the bargain but there we are...'

'Haven't kept my side of the bargain?'

Jake felt a flash of guilt. Leaving her agency was his trump card but he hadn't realised she was the company and so would likely take something like this personally.

'It's not my fault if you don't like any of the dates I've arranged for you,' she responded tartly. 'Each and every one of them is lovely and accomplished and frankly it says a lot more about you that you're not interested in a single one of them.'

Jake sat up straighter in his office chair. Wow, this woman had some fight in her.

'If you genuinely want someone to accompany you on this business trip, I'm happy to discuss it with my clients, to see if anyone might be available. But they are all busy with their own lives and so asking people to take time off with almost no notice is going to prove difficult.'

'Precisely. That's why you need to be the one to come along. Think of it as doing something public-spirited for your clients – sparing them having to endure a week with me.'

He heard her make a grunt in agreement and choked back a laugh, so as not to infuriate her still further.

'On the plus side,' he added, 'I have a feeling my next date could be a lot more interesting than the ones I've had so far.'

This comment was pointedly ignored.

'My offer is very generous, plus I only need you to accompany me to events across a few days. My team will ensure you have office space and any equipment you need, to continue with your own work the rest of the time. There will be an allowance for clothing and anything else you need, which you're welcome to keep afterwards. If the week goes well, I will write you a glowing review and post it on my social media accounts.'

Five days with this firecracker who would no doubt challenge him every step of the way; he could hardly wait! As a young model turned movie star, Jake had been driven and passionate about his work. The feeling had stayed with him throughout his career, until his personal life had spun out of control. Since then, nothing had inspired him and he wondered if he had any fight left. Until now.

He read out the figure. Despite it being a large sum of money, it was unlikely to swing the deal, so for good measure he added: 'If you still don't want to, then fine. I understand. Another agency was in touch with my team recently. You've probably heard of them. I've got the details here somewhere, let me have a look a moment…'

Her sharp intake of breath told him all he needed to know.

'It's still not feasible,' CJ said, though she seemed to be wavering. 'I can't go on a date with you, I run the dating agency. How would that look to my clients?'

'Well, it isn't really a date. It's accompanying me to some important business events. Besides, who's going to know?'

CJ laughed. 'What are you talking about? You're one of the most famous people on the planet. Everyone's going to know.'

She was right – who was he trying to kid?

'OK, so you tell them that as all of my dates have been unsuccessful so far, some face-to-face meetings with me to assess my personality are what's needed. It's what your clients would expect, after all.'

He already had an idea of what she thought of his personality. But finally she gave a heavy sigh and he knew he'd won this round. Negotiations and arrangements concluded, the call ended and he leaned back in his chair, hands behind his head.

It was then the doubts started to creep in. This was rash, for sure. He frowned as he stared at the still-open web page. Should he cancel? After all, nothing good ever came from business deals where emotions were allowed to get in the way.

Longing, more like.

Jake felt a stirring he'd not encountered in a long while – and if he got that just from a website photo and a short phone call with CJ Connors, what would it be like when he met her for real?

Maybe he should call her back, tell her it was a joke? But that would make him look like a right idiot and strangely, he didn't like the idea of her thinking that. Though he was pretty certain her current view of him was hardly glittering.

It was too late. The deal was done and CJ Connors would be spending the next week with him, whether he liked it or not. He just had to hope it wouldn't be a complete disaster.

CHAPTER 6

Long after the call had ended CJ was still staring blankly at the wall. Had that really happened? Somehow, she'd agreed to fly out to some island at the weekend, to spend five days with Jake Masterson?

Many women would give their eye teeth to have such an offer, but not her. Should she call him back and tell him that no, she wasn't going to be pushed into accompanying him and if he wanted to try some rival companies, well good luck? CJ picked up her phone but stopped short of pressing the button to return the call.

Bottom line was the psychologist in her was intrigued. Jake sounded like a mix of demanding and desperate and she wanted to know more. Besides, hadn't she been complaining about not finding him the right date because they'd not met face to face? But it was the way he suggested it, so damned arrogant! As if she should be grateful for his offer. Just for that, she wanted to say 'no'.

Conflicted, she rang her mum, expecting her to talk her out of it. Far from it.

"It must be fate. We wanted you to have a break and hey presto! one appears. Check the arrangements through with his office, and assuming it's all above board, you should go. Make sure you let us know that you've arrived safely. And CJ, try to have some fun."

Exasperated, she messaged Lauren. Her friend was sensible and would no doubt think it was totally ridiculous to be some sort of Blind Date Plus 1. She would make her realise that however attractive the offer was – both financially and in terms of her business – there was no way she should agree to it.

While she waited for a reply, there was work to get on with. There were more important clients than a demanding superstar.

The beep of her phone brought her back to reality and she realised she'd been re-reading the same sentence in an email, without taking it in.

Lauren's reply made her eyebrows rise.

'OMG mate, a trip to a beautiful island with the Jake Masterson! No-brainer, you HAVE to go. Obvs assuming there's nothing dodgy? PS do you need me to come along and carry your bags? L xx'

CJ frowned. She'd been hoping someone would talk her out of it, even though deep down she was too intrigued to pass up the offer. It seemed her mum and Lauren felt the same way. But the fact Jake had even suggested the trip – demanded she come with him – enraged her.

She paced up and down as she thought things through and sure enough, an idea started to form.

Just because she was agreeing to go, didn't mean to say she had to make it easy for him. First off, she'd take him up on his offer of covering her clothing expenses and would go on a shopping spree. And when she arrived, she was under no obligation to even be polite to him. No, by the time this trip was over, Jake Masterson was going to rue the day he had ever asked her to come with him.

***

Despite her best efforts to hate everything about it, the journey was exciting. A sleek, dark limousine arrived at her home to collect her, much to the astonishment of her neighbours. She would have preferred to spend longer in the luxurious car but they soon arrived at a private airfield. Waiting, its rotor blades swirling, was a black and gold helicopter. CJ had never been in a helicopter before and it was better than she'd ever imagined, lifting smoothly off the ground before soaring above the town and countryside. Her face was pressed to the window for the whole journey along the southern coast of England. Eventually, they reached the tip of Cornwall and continued over the sea, away from the mainland.

Soon she saw the Isles of Scilly scattered below, both the larger inhabited islands and the smaller ones, with spits of rock and land dotted between. The white beaches and aqua seas were beautiful and had she fallen asleep on the way here, she would've thought she'd woken up in the Caribbean. For a moment, she forgot all about the annoying Jake Masterson who had more or less forced her to spend a week in this archipelago paradise.

They landed at a small airport on one of the larger islands. A man was waiting for her with a Land Rover and took her luggage, while she clambered aboard.

'Welcome to St Mary's,' he said.

The next leg of her journey was short as they crossed the pretty island, with beaches, coves and lush countryside seemingly at every turn.

Once again CJ tried not to be impressed.

The Brodia St Mary's was an imposing sight at the top of the island, overlooking the harbour and sea below. CJ ducked her head as she entered the old reception area and dumped her handbag noisily onto the desk.

'CJ Connors for Jake Masterson...please.' Despite her determination to be difficult, she never forgot her manners.

'Mr Masterson's out,' the receptionist replied coolly.

'Out?'

A nod.

'He was expecting me. Are you sure?'

'Quite sure. I saw him go myself.'

Was it CJ's imagination, or did the receptionist sound breathy as she talked about the star? No wonder she was so certain of his movements.

'And no message for me?' As the words came out of her mouth, CJ realised it made her sound a bit desperate.

The receptionist shook her head lightly. 'No, I specifically asked him if there was anything he needed and he made no mention of your arrival.'

'Well perhaps you could show me to my room and let me know when he deigns to return,' CJ responded tartly. 'Oh, and I have rather a lot of luggage in the Land Rover, is there someone who can take it there for me?'

CJ's hackles rose because the receptionist was barely able to hide her glee that the new guest had been left waiting. It was bad enough having to come here at all, now she came across as some sort of needy fan. Though she was right about her belongings – when Jake had said she could buy new clothes and he'd meet the cost, she'd taken him at his word. As a result, she had plenty of new outfits to wear.

'And I don't feel one iota of guilt about it,' she muttered.

'I'm sorry did you say something?' asked the receptionist.

'Oh nothing, nothing at all,' CJ swallowed down her irritation and gave a genuine smile. None of this was the receptionist's fault after all, despite the fact that she seemed pleased Jake wasn't there to meet her. 'If someone can get my bags that would be great but otherwise, I'll find my own way to the room. Thanks.'

The scent of lilies hit her as soon as she walked through the door into the suite. They were in a large, white vase, on a plinth beside a plump, pale blue sofa. But it was the view which attracted her attention, looking out over the sea towards the uninhabited island of Samson. It was truly stunning and she opened the French doors onto the garden, which stretched towards the edge of the cliff. Stepping outside, she surveyed the magical scene for a time, before closing her eyes and breathing in the salty, fresh air.

'This is heaven,' she murmured.

'Glad you approve.'

CJ jumped and spun round to find herself face-to-face with the billionaire heartthrob, Jake Masterson.

Sally was right, he was even better looking in real life, as gorgeous as the view she'd been admiring. He'd swapped the linen suit of his publicity photos for a loose white cotton shirt and jeans. The shirt was only buttoned up halfway and, coupled with the billowing breeze, it gave CJ a tantalising glimpse of his tanned, taut chest. It was all she could do to resist reaching out and placing her hand on the smooth skin. As she looked up into those lovely brown eyes, he raised a questioning eyebrow and she felt her cheeks burn. Could he read her mind?

'You startled me, what do you mean by creeping up on people?' she demanded, trying to cover up her embarrassment.

'I did knock a couple of times,' he protested. 'The door was open so I stuck my head in and called out, but you seemed to be miles away. I didn't mean to invade your privacy but wanted to say hello and check everything was to your satisfaction?'

'No, everything is not to my satisfaction,' she put her hands on her hips. 'I turned up and you weren't even here, despite the fact I'm stuck for nearly a week with you, against my will.'

'I'm sorry to hear that,' he drawled lazily.

Even though they were outside in the spring breeze, the atmosphere around them fizzed and sparked. Was it just his film-star looks which made her feel this way, or something more? Their eyes locked, pale green meeting hazel brown and a shiver ran through her.

To her astonishment he stepped closer, a hair's breadth away and she could see him studying her lips. For a moment it seemed as if he might kiss her and she could feel flutters of excitement in her chest – but at the last second, he leant down close to her ear.

'We'd better make the most of this week, don't you think?' he whispered, the lightness of his breath on her neck sending tingles down her spine.

She turned her face to his and the action of doing so caused their lips to be a millimetre apart. CJ knew she should push him away but his closeness, the scent of him, was intoxicating. What would it be like to have his mouth on hers, have him wind his fingers into her hair, feel his firm body pressed against her…?

CJ swallowed hard and took a step back. Was it her imagination or was he too struggling to keep his desires in check?

Don't be ridiculous. He's a famous movie star – he's probably used to lots of women looking at him this way. This is merely a game to him.

Embarrassed by her reaction, CJ tore her gaze away from his, but Jake touched her elbow gently and it sent a frisson sparking through her veins. She glanced up, at him.

'An interesting start,' he said softly. 'It's good to see you aren't that disappointed to be here, after all.'

Was that meant to be a joke, to lighten the heavy atmosphere which threatened to envelop them, or was he just being damned arrogant?

'Dream on,' she retorted, lifting her chin haughtily.

He chuckled.

Resisting the urge to give him a hard shove, she folded her arms. 'So now we're both here, what's the plan?' Getting back to business seemed to CJ like the best idea.

'The first event starts at 4pm,' he said matter-of-factly. 'It's a wedding, so right up your street I'd think. It's also on one of the off-islands so I'll pick you up in good time.'

'We're going to someone's wedding?' cried CJ. She was still recovering from the whirlwind of emotions Jake's arrival had caused, and now he was dropping this bombshell.

'Did I not say?'

He knew full well he hadn't mentioned it. It wasn't the kind of thing she would have forgotten.

'Yes, we're off to watch some poor man have his ball and chain well and truly attached.' With a hearty laugh at his own joke, Jake turned on his heel and walked out of the suite, leaving a shaken CJ in his wake.

She wasn't the only one. Despite his efforts to appear calm and collected, Jake was anything but. Did she realise the impact she'd had on him in a few short minutes?

First surprise of the afternoon had been to discover that she'd actually turned up, because he'd half expected her not to. He'd found himself hurrying along to her suite and with her back to him, he'd been able to study this titian-haired woman as he approached. She was wearing flats and was around 5ft 7. Dressed in black jeans, her legs looked long and toned. She was wearing a deep green silk shirt, which pressed against the outline of her body in the sea breeze. He liked what he saw. She looked content in her own skin.

He'd watched her for a few moments, drinking her in, before pulling himself together and stepping out to say hello. When she'd spun around, her beauty had floored him and it had taken all his willpower not to step forward and kiss her, instead whispering in her ear at the last second. As he'd done so, he'd gazed at the soft nape of her neck, pressing his hands against his sides because he didn't trust himself not to reach out and touch her – which would have been wholly wrong.

Jake didn't like the feelings CJ was conjuring up; not one little bit. He was starting to regret ever inviting her here.

Question was, what was he going to do about it?

CHAPTER 7

'Damn it!'

Jake was fumbling with his gold cufflinks. Unusually, he couldn't get them through the cuffs of his dress shirt and he knew exactly who was to blame – CJ Connors.

Even when he was much younger, enjoying the first heady feelings of attraction and love, he'd never felt a rush like this. He'd spent all this time shutting his emotions away and now she'd come along and re-opened old wounds.

'Bottom line – it was a dumb idea, to invite her,' he muttered. 'This is real life, not some sort of game.'

'What's a game, Daddy? Are we going to do something together?'

Jake looked up from his sleeve, to where a pretty, blonde-haired girl was standing in the adjoining doorway.

'You don't miss a trick, do you Xanthe?' he laughed. 'But you've arrived just at the right moment. Come and give me a hand with my cufflinks, will you?'

Xanthe Masterson came across the room and he drew her close to him, kissing the top of her head tenderly.

She looked up into his face, her blue eyes – which were like her mother's – dancing with life. 'What was that for?'

'Can't I give my favourite girl a kiss?'

'Uh-oh. That means you're going to tell me something I won't like.'

'Oh really?' he roared, bending down and tickling her in the ribs.

She struggled away, peals of laughter filling the room. Jake was never happier than when he was with his beloved daughter. Xanthe was the sole person with full access to his heart and he had every intention of keeping it that way. Their relationship was so simple; they loved each other wholeheartedly, had an unbreakable bond and there were no other complications. He was well aware that once Xanthe became a teenager things might become more challenging, but thankfully he still had a few years until she reached that stage.

Jake spent the next few minutes chasing her around the room, catching her occasionally and throwing her over his shoulder, while she squealed with excitement.

'Now then,' he growled, using the same villainous tone he'd used in his portrayal of the baddie in his last film. 'If you want to be released today, young captive, then you have a task you must complete.'

'What task?'

'Help me do up my cufflinks.' He put her down and she set to work, deftly hooking the gold into place.

'There, one done,' she said proudly.

'Great, thank you.'

'What time's the wedding?'

Jake glanced at his Bremont watch. 'In a couple of hours.'

'Can't I come?'

'Sweetheart, I would love to take you with me, but it starts late and ends late. I can't get back from the island until way past your bedtime.'

'Pppplllllleeeaaasse!' she implored, looking up at him. 'It's the weekend.'

'Too late, even for a weekend. But I promise we'll do something nice together soon.' He kissed the tip of her nose and ruffled her hair.

She huffed but carried on with the task in hand.

Jake felt a pang of guilt. It had crossed his mind that he could take Xanthe to the wedding and business meetings. In many ways she'd make the perfect Plus 1, but he'd dismissed the idea because she'd be bored to tears within minutes. Instead, he needed to ensure there was time in his schedule to do something fun with her before they left the islands.

She finished the second cuff off with a flourish. 'All done. You look handsome. If I were the bride, I'd marry you.'

'Well, I won't tell the groom, but thank you. That's the best compliment I could ever have,' he laughed, scooping her into a big hug. 'Now, you remember Brooke, the nice lady who runs the hotel? You get to hang out with her for the rest of the day. Don't stay up too late, OK, or eat too much chocolate? I know you'll try to run rings around her.'

As well as being the manager, Brooke Delaney was part of the famous family which owned the global Brodia hotel chain. Jake had stayed in many of them over the years and got to know the family well. He particularly liked Brooke; she was straightforward and good-humoured and Jake was glad to find her in charge of this hotel. She and Xanthe got on immediately and she was more than happy to help out.

'I promise, I won't trick her and accidentally stay up late,' Xanthe said, returning the hug but with a twinkle in her eye.

'Butter wouldn't melt,' Jake said, as he straightened his bow tie, picked up his jacket and headed out for the short walk to the harbourside.

His original plan was to travel in the car with CJ, but he wanted to put some space between them. She was bringing up all sorts of feelings which he could do without, so it was better to only spend time with her when there were other people around.

Will, one of Jake's team, had travelled to the islands in order to hire a boat for the occasion. He'd obviously had fun with it because it was covered in colourful bunting, with lanterns and large cushions scattered around the deck, presumably for the journey back later. Jake grimaced. He didn't want Miss Connors getting any romantic ideas and thinking he'd arranged this for her. This was purely a business arrangement and by this time next week it would be concluded. It was a just few days – he could handle that, couldn't he?

The water was flat calm and full of bobbing boats. Jake had visited many places around the world and this lovely island had seriously impressed him. He made a mental note to return one day, when duty didn't call. The sun was starting to descend – it was the perfect evening for his friend's wedding and despite the quip he'd made to CJ about a 'ball and chain', he was genuinely delighted for the happy couple.

'Oh wow.'

Will's exclamation broke into his thoughts and he followed his gaze. Walking along the wide harbour wall towards them was CJ. She was wearing a three-quarter length, teal dress, cut on the bias; flattering her figure, the material flowing with her every step. Her titian hair was swept up into a French bun, her ivory skin glowing in the spring sunshine. As she walked along the harbourside heads were turning. Jake was transfixed.

CJ spotted him and waved. 'Will this do?' she asked, giving a twirl.

'You bet,' said Will and Jake gave him a sharp look.

'This is Will, he's taking us over to the island and thought it would be fitting to decorate the boat,' Jake told her, hurriedly.

'Oh, what an amazing job you've done.' CJ flashed him a big smile and Will seemed to melt under her gaze.

Jake felt a flash of irritation. 'We don't want to be late, we'd better get going.'

He put out his hand to help CJ down the stone steps to the boat, before Will had the chance. The moment he touched her smooth skin, he felt ripples of desire pulse through him.

This was not good.

He'd felt disappointed that despite the women he'd met through CJ's agency being accomplished and good company, he'd felt nothing for them; there was no chemistry. He'd begun to fear he might never feel anything again, and that had saddened him – but now he realised it wasn't the case. At this moment he wished more than anything that he felt nothing for CJ Connors; because he felt irresistibly drawn to this spirited redhead and he didn't like it at all.

Serves you right for playing with fire.

CJ wondered why Jake's jaw was taut and he was staring resolutely out to sea. It couldn't be the dress, she'd worn it to Mabe's wedding last year and everyone had said how perfect it was. So why was he cool and distant, when he'd been anything but at their meeting earlier? Maybe this is what her clients experienced; a warm welcome, followed by aloofness and distance. Well, who cared? She would focus on the wonderful scenery instead.

Will took the helm, and the boat inched its way out of the harbour. Soon they were speeding across the water towards the island of St Martin's and the wedding of Jake's good friend Sam Kerchavel.

CHAPTER 8

CJ was surprised that the celebrity wedding of wealthy property developer Sam Kerchavel and his renowned artist wife, Tara Hemsworth, was so down to earth.

The bride looked stunning in a simple, elegantly cut, floor-length white silk gown. It had a boat neck, the edging of which was encrusted with sparkling diamonds. A small train trailed behind her. Tara's long blonde hair was curled and hung loose around her shoulders. She wore a tiara, scattered with matching diamonds and delicate seashells, no doubt found on the beaches nearby. She carried a simple bouquet of yellow daffodils which brought the theme of springtime and new beginnings to the occasion.

CJ turned to look at the groom, Sam. His eyes had not left his beautiful bride, and the pride and emotion showed in his face. CJ felt the love radiating from the couple and she had to look away, for fear that a tear of happiness would roll down her cheek, even though she'd never even met them. The last thing she wanted was for Jake Masterson to realise she was enjoying herself.

Following Tara down the aisle were two maids of honour, one an older lady with short grey hair, the other around Tara's age, her blonde hair cropped short.

'Who are they?' CJ heard the guests next to her ask someone else.

'One's Tara's good friend, Annabel. She lived with her for a while when she first arrived here. I think Annabel was friends with Tara's late mother.'

'And the other?'

'Ah, that's Laura. We'd better mind how we go today, because she's the police sergeant on the islands.'

Walking between Laura and Annabel, CJ was surprised to see a large German Shepherd dog, wearing a sparkling, diamante collar. She made a mental note to ask Jake whose dog it was later, but she didn't have to wait that long. Partway through the ceremony there was a slight gasp among many of the guests, followed by a ripple of laughter. It came at the point when Sam declared his full name, of Samson.

'What's so funny?' CJ whispered to Jake.

'Tara's dog is called Delilah. You know the Bible story? Samson lost his strength and power because Delilah cut off his hair. Tara and Sam broke up for a few years and she got the dog during that time – I think she named her Delilah for fun, not expecting Sam to come back into her life.'

'Whoops.' CJ giggled.

'Exactly. I don't think she imagined the names would crop up at her wedding.'

Soon Sam and Tara were declared husband and wife. As the pair kissed tenderly, the whole room erupted into applause and cheers.

Once again CJ found herself blinking back happy tears. Even her cool companion seemed to have warmed during the occasion.

'What did you think of it? I expect you've been to quite a few ceremonies in your line of work?' Jake asked afterwards as they drank the finest French champagne in the hotel gardens. The sun was setting, sending orange hues across the manicured lawns.

'It was lovely,' CJ's face lit up. 'She looked so beautiful and they are both so in love. It was adorable.'

'Hmmmnnnhh,' said Jake, taking a big gulp from his glass.

'What does that mean?' she felt irritated by his reaction. 'Oh, I get it, you're thinking about him having his ball and chain attached. According to you, his life is now officially over.'

'Something like that.' Jake took another swig of champagne, without looking at her.

'Bit of a cynical reaction don't you think? When Sam is obviously so happy.'

Jake shrugged, infuriating CJ even more.

'What is it, Jake? Don't you believe in love?'

'I did,' he said sharply, before turning and walking away.

The strength of his reaction shocked CJ but everything fell into place. Of course. Jake Masterson had never got over losing his wife.

She tried to remember the details surrounding their tragic story. Jake had married young and CJ remembered photos of his glamorous wife, Melissa. They'd had a daughter together – that much CJ knew from the paperwork she'd received when he'd joined the agency. It had said he was a widower but she already knew that because Melissa's tragic accident had been plastered all over the news at the time. What had happened to her? CJ searched her memory for the detail. That was it, a horse-riding accident. When? Three, four years ago?

It had been a terrible tragedy for sure, but when his office had called and asked CJ to arrange some dates, she'd assumed he felt ready to move forward. Yet none of the dates had worked out and this was probably why. It was too painful for him still.

'Coming to a wedding was probably the last thing you needed,' she whispered to his retreating figure.

No wonder he was putting up barriers. She left him alone with his thoughts for a few minutes, but as she didn't know anyone else there, and had no intention of spending the evening on her own, she walked over to where he was standing, grim-faced and looking out to sea.

'I'm sorry,' she said gently, putting a hand on his arm. 'It must be tough losing the person you love.'

He turned to look at her, his handsome face full of hope, and the emotional connection she'd felt when they first met, returned. Then his face clouded over and a mask was slipped smoothly back into place.

'What do you know of it?' he asked sullenly.

CJ was taken back to the recent time in the hospital, her mum sitting beside her, white-knuckled as she clutched her handbag, her brother pale and silent on the other side of the bed. Waiting for the doctor had been agony, and she could still feel the surge of relief which flooded through her when they had learned that Grandpa was through the worst. He had taken on the role of dad when their own father had moved away and the thought of losing him was unbearable.

CJ swallowed back a sob. 'You're right, nothing thankfully, I've been extremely lucky. I can only imagine how horrible it is.'

'Oh, really?'

Something in his tone made her think better of replying.

'Well, CJ, you don't know the half of it. You don't know what true misery is, despite what your over-active imagination might tell you.'

The words stung; hurt quickly turning to irritation. Sure, she'd been lucky not to suffer his loss and couldn't imagine what it was like to no longer have his partner by his side, but she was trying to help and his reaction was uncalled for. After all, he was the one who'd demanded she accompany him here.

'Whatever you're feeling, it doesn't give you the right to be rude,' she said sharply. 'And frankly, if you're so damned anti-relationships, why on earth did you go on dates with those other women? And come to that, why did you invite me here?'

'I didn't invite you, I hired you.'

CJ gasped, her green eyes widening with shock. She wasn't going to take that from anyone, least of all a jumped-up film star.

'Fine with me,' she retorted angrily.

'What is?' He looked at her sharply.

'Fine, that you think you hired me. Because it means I can consider myself fired – and believe me, right now that feels great.'

CHAPTER 9

CJ slammed her glass down on a table, not caring that champagne sloshed everywhere. Then she turned and walked away through the bustling crowd of guests and back towards the quay where the boat had docked. She would ask Will to take her back to St Mary's and if that wasn't possible, she'd sit and chat with him until it was time to leave. Anything to get away from the horrible Jake Masterson.

'First thing in the morning, I'm out of here. He can go to another agency and tell the world how I failed him, or do what the hell he likes. As long as I don't ever have to spend another minute with him again,' she raged. 'How dare he speak to me like that, especially when I was just trying to be sympathetic.'

She heard footsteps approaching quickly from behind.

'CJ. CJ, wait up!'

She ignored him and carried on walking, until he took hold of her arm lightly and pulled her round to face him.

'What do you want?' she snapped.

'Don't. Don't go back.'

The mask had gone and Jake had an earnest look on his face but CJ was in no mood to be mucked around. She shook herself free of his grasp.

'You've got to be joking. Do you honestly think I'm going to go back there with you?' Her green eyes flashed with fury. 'How dare you treat me this way? At least now I understand why you didn't want second dates with any of the gorgeous, talented women I put forward. You don't actually want anyone, you've just been messing everyone around all this time. Go to another agency if you like and talk to the press too, though I'm sure they'll be interested to hear my side of the story. I really don't care. In the meantime, I'm out of here.'

And with that she carried on marching towards the boats.

'Whoa, whoa,' he called out.

She ignored him but could hear him hurrying to catch up.

Next, he was trotting beside her. 'I'm sorry, really sorry. It was wrong of me.'

'Which bit, being incredibly rude when I was trying to sympathise, or the line about 'hiring' me? Perhaps going on dates when you don't mean it? Or just this whole trip?'

'All of it,' he said, imploring. 'All of it was wrong. I've behaved badly. Please, accept my apology and come back to the reception?'

'I don't know, I'm going to have to think about it,' CJ bristled, stopping and turning to face him.

Somewhere nearby an owl hooted softly, as darkness started to envelop the island.

'You do know that you don't need a woman hanging on your arm anymore; this isn't the Dark Ages? There's no shame in going to an event on your own.'

'I know. And just for the record, I'm not some kind of dinosaur.'

CJ snorted but undeterred, Jake continued. 'But I want…no, I would like it if you would come back with me to the wedding reception, CJ. Please.'

CJ was wavering and it made her cross. She shouldn't even be considering changing her mind and instead should tell Jake Masterson what he could do with his invitation. 'Why should I return with you? And don't you dare say 'because I'm paying you'.'

'Wouldn't dream of it. To be honest CJ, I can't think of a single reason why you should come back with me and I'd understand perfectly if you wanted to go home. But I would like the opportunity to demonstrate that my apology is genuine.'

He held out his hand, his brown eyes soft in the last light of the day. It was like some kind of spell surrounded them both and CJ felt her resolve weakening. Besides, she did really want to go back to the reception, though she was conflicted because she should take a stand. She hesitated for a few moments and then, pointedly ignoring Jake's hand, started to walk back the way she had just come, her arms folded across her body.

Jake fell in beside her, relief flooding through him. She might be keeping six feet away from him but at least CJ hadn't left. When she spoke again, it was so quiet that he had to strain to hear her:

'You should remember that other people have been through things too. Some quite recently as it so happens. It's not all about you.'

Jake considered himself well and truly told, and inwardly reprimanded himself again. He was stunned by this powerful woman and liked that she stood up to him. She was totally right; he'd behaved badly. His mum's face popped into his mind and he wondered what she'd have said about his bad behaviour. Quite a lot, he expected and none of it good.

He was deep in thought as they approached the reception. Something had happened to CJ recently and he wondered what it was. Worse, he realised he had a sudden urge to find out and everything else about her too.

CHAPTER 10

CJ hoped none of the other guests noticed them sneak in late for the wedding breakfast. She was concerned that it appeared as though she and Jake had been outside for romantic reasons, yet the complete opposite was true.

I'm not sure I've ever met someone who's annoyed me quite so much, and certainly not this quickly, she thought as she took her seat.

Fortunately, everyone else seemed mesmerised by the exquisite banquet which was being served; delicate twice-baked cheese soufflé decorated with edible flowers, followed by smoked salmon, with sea salt and vodka cubes, plus a lemon fondant. The main course was locally reared beef which had been transformed into a Moroccan-inspired Beef Wellington. Finally, each guest received their own mini cake stand filled with an array of delicious desserts, the lower plate reserved for local cheeses – Yarg, Cornish Blue and Cornish Kern.

'There is dancing later, isn't there?' CJ asked.

'I imagine so, why?' Jake raised a questioning eyebrow.

'I need something to keep me awake. After that lovely food I could quite happily have a little snooze,' she said, patting her stomach. 'But I couldn't leave a morsel, it was way too delicious.'

He roared with laughter and she found herself joining in, for the first time enjoying an easy connection with him.

There was indeed dancing, courtesy of a fabulous big band. They played everything from Glenn Miller, right up to modern day club classics with their own twist. The first dance was reserved for the bride and groom, who swirled around the dance floor expertly to the delight of their guests and the occasional bark from Delilah.

Afterwards, others started to join in. CJ would usually be one of the first on the floor, kicking off her heels and dancing the night away, but this time she held back because she didn't know anyone. Jake didn't seem to be in a rush and she wondered if he was one of those men who didn't dance.

'Jake. So glad you're here.'

CJ was startled to find Sam Kerchavel at their table. Jake rose and the pair embraced warmly.

'Congratulations,' Jake said. 'Tara looks absolutely stunning.'

'She does, doesn't she,' agreed Sam, glancing across at his bride, who was making her way towards them. 'I'm a very lucky man.'

'You certainly are.'

'But Jake, you've not introduced me to your guest.'

'This is CJ Connors. CJ, Sam.'

CJ stood and shook hands with the well-known businessman. She was glad she'd met a few of the rich and famous before, because otherwise the sheer number in the room tonight could be overwhelming. It was like a Who's Who of people who regularly appeared on her social media and news feeds.

'It's lovely to meet you,' she said warmly. 'And many congratulations to you both.'

Tara Kerchavel reached them and Jake leaned forward to kiss her on the cheek. Introductions were made. The two men started to talk and Tara tucked her arm conspiratorially into CJ's.

'I must say, it's lovely to see Jake out on the dating scene again, good for you for managing it. Sam says he's been trying to encourage him for the past few months but to no avail.'

'Oh, well…I…' CJ was at a loss as to what to say and felt a complete fraud. What should she tell Tara? That she owned the dating agency Jake was enrolled with, but he wasn't actually interested in any of her clients? Or that he'd hired her to come to their wedding? Whatever she said would sound crass and dishonest.

'We thought we might have to give up on him, altogether. He's not seemed interested in settling down, but I guess we should've figured that, what with the affair and everything.'

CJ gave a little gasp at Tara's words. Jake had had an affair? That could explain why he was always blowing hot and cold on dates. She'd been at the sharp end of his behaviour too; one minute he was the epitome of charm, the next arrogant and dismissive. Maybe that was just the man he was. And he'd seemed wretched earlier, so perhaps there was some guilt thrown in as well? What a mess.

It brought back some unhappy memories for her too, ones she would rather forget.

'I can't believe we're actually married!' Tara continued. 'A year ago I would never have dreamed this was even possible. It just goes to show that you never know what might be on the horizon, including love.'

CJ nodded and made a mental note to remind some of her clients of that. She believed in love for others but it wasn't for her, not after her last experience. This news about Jake merely served to remind her why she'd ploughed all of her time into building her business over the past year.

'Great band.' She turned back to Tara.

'Isn't it – they're so good. Aren't you dancing?'

'Well, I would but…I don't know many people and…'

'We'll soon fix that,' Tara said determinedly. She moved across to her husband and slipped an arm gently around his waist, which immediately caught his attention. 'Sam, let Jake go, CJ wants to dance.'

CJ sighed inwardly. It was true that she had wanted to hit the dance floor earlier but now she knew about Jake's secret, well she wasn't so sure. What did she really know of him? He'd seemed like someone who was trustworthy, if a little mixed up, but Tara's revelation made her doubt that. The problem was he was so damned intoxicating and she couldn't trust herself not to fall for his easy charm. That could spell disaster.

'No honestly, I don't mind,' she said.

Jake was studying her, a look of curiosity on his face. Given their disagreement earlier in the evening, he must have wondered why she seemed keen to dance with him. Unless it was an excuse to subtly kick him in the shins, or stamp on his toes, of course. Which was tempting.

'I know my orders,' he said to the newlyweds. 'C'mon then CJ.' He gestured towards the dance floor.

A bit of dancing isn't going to hurt, is it?

She stood and threaded her way through the tables. Jake had slipped off his jacket and bow tie at the end of the meal and had undone the top couple of buttons of his shirt. As he pulled her to him, CJ found herself pressed against his chest and was trying not to stare at his smooth, tanned skin. Once again, she thought how she would like to reach out and touch it, feel the warmth of him beneath her finger tips. But how could she feel attracted to him after what she'd discovered from Tara and the way he had spoken to her? Swallowing hard, she focussed on the music instead.

Whilst he was broad and muscular, there was also a suppleness about Jake she discovered, as he expertly whirled her around the floor. His white shirt accentuated his tan, his blond, cropped hair constantly changing colour beneath the multicoloured lights, while his eyes were like dark pools – pools a girl could easily drown in.

Despite all her misgivings, she was beginning to enjoy herself. Well, where was the harm?

They danced almost non-stop for a couple of hours, twirling and laughing, oblivious to everyone else in the room and the looks they were receiving. CJ was glad she'd taken dance classes over the years because Jake was good. Then she remembered he'd danced in a couple of his films. Together they danced the night away, only missing a number to quench their thirst, or catch their breath.

'Are you enjoying yourself?' he asked during one of their breaks.

She nodded.

Yet Jake felt unconvinced. Perhaps it was the row they'd had at the beginning of the evening which was still casting a shadow over things? He shook the thought away.

CJ was certainly a match for him on the dance floor and he was mesmerised by her grace. Her teal dress swirled and sashayed like a flamenco dancer's with her every step, giving him tantalising glimpses of her long legs. Her copper hair was ablaze under the lights and he was left in no doubt of her stamina, as she kept pace with him in every number. She was simply dazzling, and it was no surprise that he could see admiring glances from some of the male guests; not that CJ seemed aware.

Finally, the end of the evening arrived and the band selected a smooth, slow number to bring the event to a close. CJ went to leave the dance floor to allow the other couples to occupy it, but Jake stepped in her way.

'Where do you think you're going?' he whispered, close to her ear. He sensed her shiver.

'It's the slow number,' she said by way of explanation.

'So?'

'So, it's for couples.'

'Well, I haven't spent the whole evening dancing with you to be ditched at the end.'

CJ raised her eyebrows. All the same, she allowed herself to be taken into his arms and immediately Jake felt conflicted again – desire mixed with an urge to run away from her intoxicating charms. He was acutely aware of the softness of her lithe body against his.

Her face was pressed against his chest and he hoped the fast beating of his heart didn't give his feelings away. Without thinking, he nuzzled his face gently into the top of her hair, breathing her scent in deeply and causing her to look up. Their eyes locked. If he wasn't careful, all the barriers he'd carefully constructed over the past few years, would come crashing down. What was he doing? He needed to get a grip.

Eventually the music came to an end, snapping them out of the moment. They stepped away from each other and an awkwardness settled there instead. CJ walked outside a few steps ahead of him, ready for the journey home.

'Did you bring a wrap or anything? It's a bit cold,' said Jake.

CJ shook her head without looking at him.

'No matter, Will has some blankets on board. In the meantime, take my jacket.'

'Oh, don't worry. I'll be fine.'

'I insist.' Jake held out the dark dinner jacket and she took it, giving him a grateful nod before slipping it over her slender shoulders. She looked swamped under the swathes of fine fabric and to Jake's horror her bottom lip started to tremble.

'CJ, are you OK?' He stepped forward and gently touched her arm, searching her face.

'I'm fine,' she hurriedly wiped away some tears onto his sleeve. 'It's that last song – so emotional, it always gets to me.'

Really? Jake was surprised. The music had ended a few minutes ago and she'd seemed fine while it was playing. Maybe it was something else? He decided to test her.

'You mean the lyrics? The elderly couple still together after all those years?'

'Exactly. Emotional words. Always gets me here,' she said, lightly thumping her chest. 'Anyway, shall we go?'

And she walked ahead of him into the darkness.

Interesting. Jake watched her go with a lopsided grin. Then without further ado, he caught up with her as they headed towards the row of brightly-lit boats.

CHAPTER 11

When CJ woke the next morning, it took her a few moments to realise where she was. She jumped up eagerly and pulled back the curtains to gaze at the view. It was a sunny day, though clouds skimmed the sky. As assignments went, this location was gorgeous, which made it even harder to remember that she was meant to be annoyed about the whole thing.

She switched on her phone, while she made herself a cup of tea, and was surprised to hear it beeping time and again. Puzzled, she picked it up.

There were four missed calls and a whole array of texts, all from her mother and grandpa. Scratch that; there were a couple from Lauren and the last message was from Tim.

CJ, PLEASE call Mum n Grandpa. They seem 2 think something's happened to you. As if. Tim xx

CJ gasped. She'd promised to give her mum a call to let her know she'd arrived safely, but in all the excitement of the wedding – no, all the drama of meeting Jake Masterson – it had completely slipped her mind. Her brother always forgot to call, but for her it was completely out of character. It said a lot about her meeting with the enigmatic businessman. She immediately brought up her mum's number.

'CJ, where have you been? We've been worried sick. I was wondering whether to call the police.'

'Oh Mum, I'm so sorry. Jake took me to a wedding on another island yesterday evening and it went on until late. I should've texted but I forgot.'

'You forgot?' The incredulity in her mum's voice said it all.

'I know, I'm sorry. Is Grandpa OK?' CJ hoped that changing the subject would put her mum off the scent, but no such luck.

'He's fine, or he will be once he knows we've spoken. But what's going on, CJ? Are you sure you're alright? I've never known you forget to call in. Your brother, well, that's a different story. But not you. And this whole trip…I know we asked you to consider having a break but this…'

She couldn't blame her mum for faltering, CJ hardly knew how to describe the visit herself.

'That Jake Masterson person,' her mother continued, this time in a whisper. 'Is he there with you now? Can he hear me?'

'Mum, of course he's not here with me now! I'm in my pyjamas in my suite. And I only met him yesterday. Give me some credit.'

Her mother ignored her indignation. 'Suite eh? Very smart.'

'It is. Lovely in fact. I think you and Grandpa would like it here, so maybe we should think about coming here sometime. But in the meantime, I have to go, Mum. I'm not sure what's planned today and I've not even had breakfast yet.'

CJ gave more reassurances about taking care of herself and keeping in touch before ending the call. Turned out her Mum had also contacted Lauren, so she had to message both her and Tim to reassure them all was well.

By the time she'd done that it was gone 8.30am, so she quickly jumped in the shower. Then she dressed, opting for navy chinos with a deep red, cotton jumper. She dried her hair and put on some mascara and a touch of lipstick.

According to the information in her room, breakfast was served in the large conservatory. As she reached the door to head out, she spotted something. It was a note, which had been slipped underneath, of which just a part was visible.

She snatched it up quickly. It was written on a piece of hotel headed paper.

Mr Masterson asks you to join him for breakfast in his suite and hopes 8.45am will suit. Best wishes, Reception

'Whoops, that was more than twenty minutes ago.' CJ read it with dismay.

She hated to be late for anything, although he'd not mentioned anything about breakfast last night.

The note gave details of how to reach his suite and so she quickly hurried there, pausing when she was a few steps away. Was it a good idea – to go alone, particularly given the affect he had on her? But it was first thing in the morning and Jake would no doubt be keen to get on with the day's work, so surely there was no harm in it?

She knocked firmly on the door.

'Aha, you got my message,' Jake opened it with a dazzling smile. 'Come on in.'

He was wearing a T-shirt which showed off his ripped abs. CJ tore her gaze away in case he saw her staring, only to look down and realise he was wearing board shorts, which showed off his tanned, strong legs. It was unfair for anyone to look that good so early in the morning.

Swallowing hard, she stepped into the room, immediately aware that he wasn't alone.

Sitting at the dining table, watching CJ, was a girl. She shared the blonde hair and broad smile of her father but her eyes were blue. The resemblance was unmistakable, this had to be…

'My daughter, Xanthe.'

Jake gestured proudly. CJ gave her a warm smile and the girl returned it cautiously.

'Xanthe, this is CJ. She's my er…she's…'

Jake faltered and CJ wasn't surprised. How was he going to explain her? His hired date, who he got to come along through near-blackmail? Not a great example for his child.

'She's my special assistant this week. Helping me out with a few business meetings.'

Standing behind her, Jake didn't see his daughter roll her eyes. CJ wondered what it meant. Was she the latest in a long line of 'special assistants'? It seemed unlikely, given Jake's miserable track record of dating. Or was it the mention of the business meetings, taking up her father's time?

'It's nice to meet you, Xanthe.'

She put out her hand.

Jake's daughter seemed surprised at this, but she reached across and shook it gently, her hand soft and light in CJ's. Her father gestured to CJ to take a seat at the table, on which was an array of food; smoked salmon, eggs, cereals, toast, pastries and freshly squeezed juice.

'I hope this is OK? Please, help yourself. Can I get you a tea or coffee?'

CJ was pleasantly surprised. When she'd read the note, she'd pictured Jake surrounded by waiting staff attending to his every need, surely part and parcel of the life of a billionaire? Yet here he was pouring her tea, and as far as she could tell, they were the only three people in the suite. She reached across for a bowl and scooped some fresh fruit into it, before topping it with creamy Greek yoghurt.

'Sorry I'm later than you suggested. I slept in and didn't notice the note until I was about to head out.' She didn't mention she'd also had to call Lauren and her family, because they were beginning to think that Jake had done away with her.

'No need to apologise. I should've thought about it last night but I was a bit distracted.'

He winked and CJ wondered what it meant.

'Anyway, I realised this morning but didn't want to wake you, so I asked one of the staff to slip a note under your door. Glad you slept so long. It must've been all that dancing.' He passed the cup of tea across to her and then took the seat next to Xanthe.

'I am pretty tired this morning, though I put it down to the sea air,' CJ grinned.

'Me too. I was looking forward to a lie-in but was disturbed by this little Miss here, leaping on top of me and bashing me over the head with a pillow.' Jake grabbed his daughter and tickled her and her giggles echoed round the room.

An image of the billionaire lying in bed, the sheets tousled around him popped into CJ's head and sent a shiver right through her. She forced herself back to the present, lest he read her mind, and focussed on his daughter instead. 'So, Xanthe, how do you like it here?'

CJ started on safe, neutral territory.

'It's really pretty, but I've not seen much. You should see the play area over there though,' Xanthe pointed away to her right. 'I've never been on swings with a view of the sea before.'

Despite CJ being a stranger, the young girl chattered away enthusiastically for a few minutes about how the play area compared with the one she had at home. CJ sipped her tea and listened carefully, admiring her confidence.

'Did you go to Uncle Sam's wedding with my dad?' Xanthe switched subjects.

'I did.'

'I asked earlier what Tara's dress was like he just said 'white'.'

CJ glanced at Jake and he shrugged.

'What can I say, I'm not that great on dresses.'

'I thought you used to be a model?'

'I was and I wore a lot of unusual and outlandish outfits, that's for sure. But never a dress, at least not that I can recall.'

'That's not what I meant.' CJ couldn't help but laugh. 'I thought having been part of the fashion world you'd have a bit of a clue and be able to describe a wedding dress at least.'

Jake splayed his hands wide. 'Hey, it was a long time ago and I didn't pay attention to what they were saying about the girls' clothes.'

'So, as he's useless, can you tell me what Tara wore?' Xanthe pleaded.

'Well luckily for you, I was paying attention and better still, I took some photos.'

For the next twenty minutes CJ shared details of the fabulous wedding with Xanthe, showing her the images she'd captured on her phone. Jake relaxed back in his chair and she was conscious of him watching her, as she chatted to his daughter.

Eventually, Jake looked at his watch and stood up. 'Sorry to spoil the glamour-chat ladies, but I have to get on with some work – I've a few things I must do. Feel free to stay here as long as you like, CJ. We've got a business lunch to attend, though not until 2pm. It's across the other side of St Mary's so I'll meet you in reception 20 minutes before?'

'I'll be there,' said CJ, finishing up her tea.

'I'm sorry the lunch is late; it can't be helped unfortunately.'

'Not a problem, it gives me time to explore the island. I've been itching to ever since I arrived.'

'What am I going to do, Dad?' Xanthe wailed, and CJ felt for her.

'Haven't you got some more school work to do? And I think there are some new Netflix films that you've not seen yet, you can check them out.'

Xanthe made a face; she obviously wasn't keen on the idea. She started to get up, reluctantly.

'You're welcome to come and explore with me if you want to, Xanthe?' CJ said, adding quickly, 'I mean, if that's OK with your dad and I'm not taking you away from your studies?'

The little girl's face brightened. 'Yes please,' she said enthusiastically. 'Can I go with CJ, Dad? It's still the weekend.'

While she was happy to take her around the island, CJ was sure Xanthe would have preferred to go with Jake. She knew exactly how she felt. Her own parents divorce happened when she wasn't much older than Xanthe and her dad soon moved away for work. He tried to spend time with her and Tim, but the relationship wasn't as close as it could've been. CJ knew it wasn't easy, particularly if you were the sole parent, but that precious time was something money couldn't buy. Did Jake spend much quality time with his daughter? Somehow she doubted it.

'It's OK with me if Xanthe goes with you, but are you sure? Wouldn't you rather look around on your own?' Jake said doubtfully.

'No, it's fine. I'd like the company,' CJ said quickly. 'It'll be fun. Xanthe, I'll meet you outside reception in 15 minutes.'

They waved goodbye at the doorway as she left the suite, Xanthe holding on tightly to her father's other arm, chatting nineteen to the dozen about her impending sightseeing tour. Jake was leaning down to her as if trying to catch every word and it made CJ smile.

Maybe he's not totally irredeemable after all. Yes, maybe there's more to Jake Masterson than meets the eye.

CHAPTER 12

CJ made her way to the meeting place to find Jake and Xanthe already there, sitting on the wall outside the front of the hotel.

'Thanks again for taking Xanthe with you. It's pretty boring for a ten-year-old having to wait for me to finish work,' Jake explained.

CJ glanced at Xanthe but her face wasn't giving anything away.

'My pleasure,' she said brightly. 'I've been keen to look around and it's better when there's someone with you. You sure you don't want to join us?'

Jake made a pained face. 'I'd love to, really I would. It sounds like a lot more fun than going through contracts and replying to clients. But unfortunately, duty calls.'

So it was that CJ and Xanthe walked down the steep road which led to St Mary's harbour.

'I've been looking online and it says the boats will be waiting to take the tourists to the off-islands. Shall we go there first and watch?' CJ asked.

Xanthe nodded in agreement.

Sure enough, down on the long, stone harbour a large group of tourists was gathered, kitted out in walking boots and colourful waterproof coats, sporting backpacks and carrying Nordic poles, ready for any weather and terrain. Spring was definitely in the air but the next landfall beyond was the USA and Canada, a few thousand miles away. It meant weather systems could change quickly. For now though, the sun poked through the clouds and there was the softest of breezes.

Down below the harbour steps, where she'd met the boat which had taken them to Sam and Tara's wedding, a row of craft was moored. Each had a couple of crew members on board and every one was scheduled to head to a different off island, or set off on one of the sightseeing trips on offer around the waters.

Xanthe and CJ watched as the visitors clambered on board and waited for the vessels to depart. Once everyone was ready, the laden boats left within minutes of each other, spreading out like a fan across the sea towards the off-islands of St Agnes, Bryher, St Martin's and Tresco. One boat remained moored in the harbour and a sign showed that it was going to head out shortly to explore areas around some of the uninhabited islands, which were a known habitat for seals.

'Oh wow,' said Xanthe, pointing to the sign. 'Seeing seals would be amazing.'

'Well, let's see if we have time tomorrow and maybe we could take your father along with us?'

'I doubt it,' Xanthe replied, morose. 'He only has time for work, not for anything else.'

CJ felt terrible for her and decided to see if she could help. Though how, she wasn't sure. Jake seemed determined and self-assured, so he'd probably see it as interfering. But she had to try, for his sake as well as Xanthe's. Maybe work had been a solace after his wife's tragic accident but Jake might forever regret not spending time with Xanthe.

The two of them moved to the other side of the harbour and watched the waves for a moment in silence. Then, rounding the tip of Tresco came a beautiful navy-hulled luxury yacht, which dwarfed the other boats.

'Look, there's Uncle Sam's boat,' Xanthe said excitedly, pointing.

'Sam Kerchavel?'

'Yes. That's his boat. It's named after his new wife, it's the Tara.'

CJ stared at the beautiful vessel. How lovely that Sam should name it after his wife.

'And he's your uncle?'

'Not my real uncle but he's good friends with my dad, so I've always called him that. He and Tara are going to stop by and see me later, I can't wait.'

Sam Kerchavel – Xanthe's 'Uncle' Sam. CJ had often wondered what it must be like to live in this world, surrounded by wealth and luxury and seemingly having no real worries. But her glimpse into Jake's life showed you were never totally immune from problems and concerns. CJ was fortunate, her business was doing well and she was passionate about it. It meant she was making a decent income but it was nothing compared with this lifestyle. Yet to Xanthe this was completely normal.

'Let's go and see what else there is here,' CJ said quickly and they headed off across St Mary's.

First, they did some window shopping in Hugh Town. Being Sunday, several of the shops were closed, giving the islanders a well-deserved day off. CJ made a mental note to pop back in a day or so to pick up a couple of surfing sweatshirts for her brother and his girlfriend. She might get one for herself too; for all the glamour of the wedding and this week's business events, she liked to be snuggled up in a warm hoodie just as much. There was also some lovely jewellery, crafted by an islander called Adrienne, which her mum would love. In the same window hung one of Tara Kerchavel's gorgeous seascape prints, which would be perfect for her sea-loving grandpa.

They reached the end of the shops and headed right, walking up some stone steps which opened out to give a view of Porthcressa beach. CJ immediately fell in love with the charming sandy cove, where the sea lapped gently against the shore.

'This is pretty,' said Xanthe, enthusiastically. 'Can I go for a paddle?'

CJ was surprised about how warm it was on the islands for the time of year, but the sea? Well, that was a totally different matter. 'I think it's going to be a bit cold but let's stick our toes in first and see.'

'You'll come in with me?' Xanthe looked up with surprise.

'Of course, I'm not missing the chance to have a paddle on a beach like this,' laughed CJ and they headed towards the water. As they removed their shoes and socks, CJ wondered at Xanthe's surprise.

She remembered an old saying: an only child is a lonely child. For a child who'd lost her mother and whose father was always tied up with his work, that would be even truer. Her thoughts were literally swept away by the sea as they tentatively put their feet in, squealing as the cool water washed over them.

'Oh wow, that's cold,' said CJ. 'But we should get used to it in a moment.'

In the end they spent half an hour in the water, allowing it to go over their ankles and feeling the soft sand shifting beneath them with every gentle pull of the waves. They paddled to an area of rocks to the left of the beach and studied some of the sea creatures who'd made their home there, such as winkles and tiny crabs.

Eventually, they headed to the café at the top of the beach where a few other visitors were sitting, taking in the view. CJ ordered a hot chocolate but Xanthe opted for an ice cream in a cone.

'An ice cream,' exclaimed CJ. 'My, you're made of tough stuff, young lady.'

Afterwards, they headed back via the cliffs, through a small copse of trees before the path opened out onto the exposed piece of headland, near the site of former military batteries, where soldiers kept watch on this part of the island hundreds of years ago. They stopped for a few moments to read about their history.

The views were stunning. The Isles of Scilly hadn't been on her list of places to visit before, but if one good thing had come from Jake's demanding she accompany him, it was that she'd got to visit such a magical place. She sighed inwardly as she realised her vow to hate everything about this trip was becoming more and more difficult; particularly the part about not letting Jake Masterson get under her skin.

CHAPTER 13

Jake yawned and stretched. Dog tired from a sleepless night of feisty CJ filling both his sleeping and waking thoughts, made concentrating on work hard going. Even though he had some important documents to review, his mind pondered what Xanthe and CJ were up to. He may as well have gone with them, for all the good he was doing here.

A smile formed on his lips. One thing was for sure, it would have been a very different day out from the ones he was used to. When his first blockbuster film came out, bringing with it fame and fortune, people developed a reverence for him which he didn't much enjoy. Only his family and close friends still told him it like it was. So, CJ was like a breath of fresh air because she certainly wasn't afraid to tell him exactly what she thought of him – good or bad. Chiefly bad.

His grin faded. Problem was, what she thought of him was starting to matter and that was dangerous. Melissa's face came to his mind and guilt once again gnawed at his stomach.

Jake tried to distract himself by pulling up the next document on his screen but before long his concentration was waning again. He picked up the photo of Xanthe which he'd placed carefully on the desk when he first arrived at the hotel. He studied the picture of his beautiful girl beaming at the camera, a strand of her blonde hair across her face. There was no way he'd risk her happiness by introducing a new dynamic into their mix.

And what was it CJ had mentioned when they'd had their falling out?

'You should remember that other people have been through things too. Some quite recently.'

What the hell did that mean?

The knock at the door, which signalled a mid-morning coffee arriving could not have been more welcome. As soon as the member of hotel staff had left, he poured himself a mug, carried it to the window and stared out to sea.

What would Xanthe and CJ be talking about now? Did his daughter think they were dating, given they'd gone to Sam and Tara's wedding together? He cursed himself for not explaining it to Xanthe himself, though exactly what he'd have said, he didn't know. She'd been through so much with the death of her mother; Jake didn't want to cause her any more pain. He ran his hand through his hair distractedly. He needed to get a grip. Slugging back the remains of his coffee he returned to his desk. This time he would get his work done, damn it!

Eventually he heard their voices outside and he jumped up hurriedly and headed to the door.

'Thank you, I've had a great time,' Xanthe was saying happily. 'And thank you for the ice cream too.'

'Ice cream, at this time of year? Are you crazy?' said Jake swinging the door open and filling the frame. CJ took a step back, seemingly startled by his appearance. He looked down and realised his shirt wasn't done up properly. No doubt his hair was a mess too. Quickly, he buttoned up, glancing back up to see that CJ was blushing and staring at her shoes. Jake grinned. Maybe her view of him wasn't all bad, after all.

'I hope that was OK.'

CJ seemed to be addressing the ground and he barely caught what she said.

'Was what OK?'

'The ice cream. I realise I hadn't thought to check before we went. We did walk around the headland so we've done a bit of exercise to work it off.'

'And we paddled for ages in the sea, Dad. It was great.' Xanthe hugged her father and looked into his face imploringly. 'Please say you'll come next time.'

'Paddling in the freezing sea in March, followed by an ice cream? OK, you're on. Wouldn't miss it for the world,' Jake laughed, squeezing his daughter's shoulder. 'Though to be fair, it's warmer here on the islands than it is at home.'

Xanthe turned and gave CJ a wave before ducking in under his arm and out of sight into the suite.

'Thank you, she seems to have had a lovely time.'

CJ seemed surprised by the tenderness in his voice. 'It was my pleasure, she's lovely. Genuinely.'

Jake brightened. He loved Xanthe with everything he'd got and thought she was a great kid, but also recognised that he was totally biased. 'I'm glad you think so and that you had a good time. Let's hope you enjoy my company just as much at our business lunch.'

'On that note, I'd better go,' CJ glanced at her phone. 'Oh my, I didn't realise it was this late. I need time to get ready.'

'Oh, I doubt that,' Jake said lazily, leaning against the door frame. He was pleased to see her flush again. 'You could probably sling on a hessian sack and pull it off. Not that I'm suggesting you wear one of those, of course.'

'Oh damn.' CJ clicked her fingers with pretend annoyance. 'That was exactly what I was planning to wear. Oh well, if I can't wear my sack, I'd better go and choose something else. See you in half an hour.'

And with that she swung her bag over her shoulder, turned on her heel and walked briskly away. As she did so, she was acutely aware of Jake watching her, every step of the way.

CHAPTER 14

The outfit CJ chose was a world away from a hessian sack – a short, exquisite pale pink dress, she'd found in a lovely boutique near her office. It was beautifully cut and the addition of a cute tassel hem gave it a sense of playfulness. She'd been unsure of it at first but Lauren had insisted she tried it on, and as soon as she'd looked at herself in the mirror in the changing rooms, she knew her friend was right. It was perfect.

Given she and Jake were going for lunch nearby and she wouldn't have to clamber on board a boat, or negotiate cliff paths, CJ decided to sling on her nude heels too.

'Wow, you make me feel under-dressed,' Jake declared, as she opened the door to him. He was joking, of course, sporting a mid-blue suit with an open-neck, white shirt.

'You're a lot taller than you were earlier, though.'

CJ laughed, and the pair headed to meet the hotel car, which carried them smoothly to the restaurant.

Three other couples joined them, all of whom she'd met at the wedding. To her left was Douglas, a semi-retired banker and next to him, his wife, Barbara. CJ soon learnt they spent most of their time on the golf course. Any fears she had about being welcomed were short-lived and in no time they were questioning her about her company, Hearts & Mind Dating.

'It's so satisfying when you put a couple together and they hit it off right away, especially if it blossoms into a long-lasting relationship,' CJ explained. 'Even if it only leads to friendship, that in itself can be life-changing for some people.'

'I expect there've been some weddings, as a result?' Douglas asked.

'Oh yes,' CJ's enthusiasm was plain for all to see. 'And one or two babies too.'

'How lovely.' Barbara's eyes shone. 'What a wonderful business to have, to be able to change people's lives for the better. And you must be pleased that it's worked so well in your case too,' she added, nodding towards Jake who was talking to the person on the other side of him. 'Did you use your magic formula on him too?'

CJ froze with horror. 'Oh no, I er…I mean we're not really…'

CJ was at a loss for words. What had Jake told his business associates about her, how had he described their relationship? She looked down at her hands, unable to meet Barbara's eye.

Fortunately, their next course arrived and they all focussed on the delicious home-produced food, which showcased the delights of Cornwall and the Isles of Scilly.

'I wanted to thank you again for spending time with Xanthe today. It meant a lot to her.' Without warning, Jake took CJ's hand and lightly brushed his fingers against her wrist, sending sparks racing through her body.

'It was a pleasure,' she spluttered, losing her appetite.

What was he doing, taking her hand, causing her to blush and making out to anyone who was looking that they were an item? She was already annoyed that Barbara and Douglas appeared to think they were together, and now Jake was adding to the illusion. She snatched her hand away quickly. He shot her a look of surprise, before taking up his spoon and fork again.

'She seemed taken with you and with the island, of course.'

'I was taken with her. Xanthe is a lovely girl,' CJ replied matter-of-factly.

'I'm glad you think so.' He turned to face her. 'I think she's great but I'm conscious that as her father, I would think that. Hence why a compliment from someone like you is a big deal.'

CJ was puzzled. Why should he care what she thought, or anyone else come to that? He was a wealthy man and didn't need to worry about others' opinions, least of all hers. They hardly knew each other, and would be going their separate ways in a few days.

'Well, you don't need to worry, she's a great kid. We had a lovely time and she obviously adores you.' CJ decided there was no time like the present to try to push the importance of the father-daughter relationship.

'Do you think?'

'It's written all over her face. She loves nothing better than being with you. Maybe she could show you some of the places we went to this morning, before you leave.'

'I'd like that – I'll see what I can do.'

If Jake knew what she was up to, he wasn't letting on and CJ tucked into her dessert feeling hopeful that her suggestion might have hit home. Her feelings were short-lived though, because while coffee was served, Jake's phone beeped. As he read the message, a frown crossed his face.

Quickly, he put the phone back into his pocket. 'I don't think there'll be much time for sight-seeing. Xanthe's tutor is coming out to the island tomorrow, so that will keep her occupied.'

Was it her imagination or was there a slight edge to his voice? The atmosphere between them had also turned chilly, but why? Surely, he didn't think CJ's suggestion of a bit of downtime would impact on his daughter's studies?

'I see,' was all she could muster in reply.

'You sound like you don't approve.' He studied her closely. 'Her tutor's one of the top in his field, used to be a teacher at a leading private school.'

CJ cast her mind back to her own sweet school and the laughter of the children in the playground which echoed all around the village. Xanthe's educational experience was very different and, top tutor or not, she knew which she preferred.

'When does she get to see her friends?' she blurted out.

Jake seemed unconcerned. 'She'll see some of her cousins soon, they live in the States and we're flying out there for a conference. And next year she'll be going to school near London, so she'll make new friends there.'

This wasn't what CJ meant, so she didn't respond.

Jake made a face. 'Look, I admit, I need to sort it out. It's just we sort of lost touch with some of her friends since…well… after…'

He faltered and CJ felt terrible for him. What had his life been like after the death of his wife? Was it any wonder he hadn't got things quite together for Xanthe? She ticked herself off for being so judgemental; he was a single dad who was no doubt doing his best, in difficult circumstances.

'I can't imagine how hard it was.'

'It was. Unbelievably tough. It took us a while to get ourselves together and as a result, we lost touch with many of our friends. I've realised recently that it's something I need to work on.'

'Well, I imagine your friends are still there for you. Maybe they're just waiting for you to reach out?'

'You know what, I think you're right.' Jake held her gaze and she felt her whole body tingle. 'I'll put in some calls when we get back, see how we go.'

CJ wanted to ask more but the gentle tapping of a spoon on a glass interrupted them, and Douglas stood up to make a short speech.

Jake was strangely quiet as he settled into the car for the short journey back to the hotel. When they got into the vehicle, his leg brushed against CJ's, sending every fibre of her being into overdrive. Quickly, she moved away and glanced at him. His face was impassive as he stared out of the window. How could that be? Surely he felt it too? If not, then she'd been imagining a connection between them. She sagged back in her seat. Was this all a game to him? Tara had mentioned an affair, after all.

When the car pulled up at the hotel entrance, CJ was out of the door like a shot, keen to put some distance between them.

'In a hurry?' Jake caught up with her and blocked her path. 'I've paid for you for the whole week, I could demand you spend the rest of the day with me. Or maybe even the night.'

CJ gasped. 'What the hell? How dare you!'

Jake's laugh was bitter and he didn't move out of the way. 'What, is the thought of spending the night with me so bad? Why not? We're both adults.'

'You've got to be kidding?' CJ clenched her fists.

'Not at all. We're both single – at least I am. We've got a few hours to kill. I don't have an issue with it if you don't.'

'Believe me, I have plenty of issues with it.' CJ didn't care that her voice was rising. 'As if I'd ever spend the night with someone like you!'

'Oh, really?' Jake's eyes glittered darkly.

'Yes, really. I came here – under duress I might add – to accompany you to some business events. That's all. If you want more, I'm sure one of your adoring fans will oblige.'

He stepped back, almost as if she'd physically struck him and she knew her words had hit home. Good. How dare he speak to her in that way? Even Angus hadn't spoken to her this badly and that was a relationship she was keen to forget.

'I don't know what's got into you,' she hissed. 'But whatever it is, it's not my problem. So, I suggest we cancel our arrangement for the week and instead you spend the time taking a long hard look at yourself.'

With that CJ pushed roughly past him and stormed off towards her room, leaving Jake in her wake.

***

Jake stood there for a long time after CJ had gone. His misplaced fury started to subside, replaced instead by a cold creeping dread in his stomach.

What had he done? He'd taken his bad mood out on her, in part lashing out because he wanted to push her away. Well, he'd done a great job, there was no way she'd want anything to do with him now. He'd insulted her in the worst possible way and she was no doubt packing her bags right now.

Instead of going indoors, Jake headed towards the cliffs, slumping onto the first bench and burying his head in his hands.

What an idiot.

At lunch he'd been feeling unsure of his footing with this new woman who'd strode so confidently into his life and he was afraid of letting her in. Now the message on his phone had made him feel worse. So, he'd spoken to CJ appallingly - again. It was so unlike him.

But as he'd watched her stride away, head held high, he realised he'd created a chasm between them and he didn't like it at all. What if she jumped on the next flight home and he never saw her again? He was shocked at how miserable that made him feel.

Jake rubbed the sides of his temples with his thumbs to get rid of a niggling headache, then looked at the spectacular view. Usually, being surrounded by such beauty calmed him, but not this time. If anything, it was making him feel worse.

The rhythmic sound of the waves did give his mind more clarity though, and he realised that above all else he had to make it up to CJ. He wanted their paths to cross in the future, but that wasn't going to happen if he didn't do something to make amends. Question was, what?

Flowers, chocolates, a decent bottle of champagne – even if he sent all three, there was no way it was going to be enough. To her it would seem like an empty gesture. No, what he needed to do was find something that was important to her.

Jake watched the rise and fall of the sea, willing it to provide inspiration. A couple of gulls circled overhead, squawking. Further down the footpath a group of walkers was approaching, and he realised he stood out like a sore thumb in his business suit, while they sported hiking boots, shorts and hats. They were coming from around the headland, much like Xanthe and CJ had done earlier. Would the day have turned out differently if he'd gone with them?

And then the idea struck him. With luck and careful handling, it might work.

Jake thought through the details for a few minutes, then offered a word of thanks into the salty breeze, and with renewed enthusiasm jumped up from the bench and headed back to the hotel to see his daughter.

CHAPTER 15

CJ woke the next morning feeling exhausted after a restless night of fractured dreams.

She reached across to her phone and switched it on. It beeped almost immediately, with a message from Lauren checking she was ok. They'd had a long talk the evening before, once CJ had realised there was no room on the last flight off St Mary's.

CJ replied to the message with a kiss and a smiley emoji, then yawning, headed for the shower. Rubbing the condensation from the mirror afterwards, she could make out her pale face and the dark rings under her eyes.

Her pale pink T-shirt and matching cardigan would likely make her look a bit less washed out and she paired them with her blue jeans. Then she dug out her concealer and did the best she could to cover up her misery. Jake's suggestion had been outrageous, yet she couldn't help but feel there was more to it. That made her cross with herself – she shouldn't be excusing his behaviour, whatever the reason behind it. Much as she'd like to see Xanthe again, there was no way she was heading to the billionaire's suite for breakfast. Instead, she set off towards the hotel restaurant.

'And after that I'm outta here,' she declared, as she strode around the corner.

'Why, where are you going?'

CJ almost bumped straight into Xanthe and Jake, who were coming the other way. They'd obviously been for a swim, both had damp hair and Xanthe was wrapped in a large towel. Jake was wearing dark boardshorts and her gaze was drawn to his tanned legs once again. His T-shirt was still damp and clung to his body, showing every rippling muscle. CJ swallowed hard and silently cursed, furious with herself for still being attracted to such a man. She turned her attention to his daughter instead.

'Oh, Xanthe, I'm sorry but I've got to head home sooner than I thought.'

'You're leaving? When?'

'I'm on the ten o'clock flight.'

'Today? But you can't! I wanted to spend some more time with you,' wailed Xanthe. She turned to her father. 'Dad, help me persuade CJ to stay.'

Jake took in his daughter's imploring face. 'It's up to CJ. Sounds like she's got good reasons for leaving.'

CJ shot him a filthy look. He'd got that right.

He seemed untroubled. 'But look, why don't you head back to the suite Xanthe, and give us a minute?'

CJ stiffened. Much as she didn't want to upset a ten-year-old, there was no way she was going to stay on this island for a moment longer. And she certainly had nothing to say to Jake.

Xanthe nodded. 'We've just been for a swim and I was telling Dad how we were paddling yesterday. I thought maybe we could go again?'

'Let me talk to your dad for a few minutes. You go on and start your breakfast. I expect you're hungry after all that swimming.'

'Yeah, I am. It was great. I dunked Dad under the water loads of times.'

'Well, that certainly does sound good,' CJ replied, a little too enthusiastically.

Jake raised an eyebrow.

Xanthe turned to go. 'CJ, please stay. And come to breakfast too.' Then she headed off in the direction of their suite.

CJ tilted her chin and crossed her arms. She didn't want to hear what Jake had to say.

'Your flight's at ten?'

'It is, and I have every intention of being on it.'

Was it her imagination or did a look of panic cross his face? It was gone almost as quickly.

'I don't expect you to cut me any slack at all after yesterday but can I put something to you, for Xanthe's sake?'

'That's really not fair on either of us.'

Jake nodded. 'I know. Look what time is it now – nearly 8am? Come and have breakfast with us and I can explain more. Then if you still want to catch your flight afterwards, well I'll even carry your bags to the car myself.'

CJ raised her eyebrows. She presumed the billionaire hadn't carried his own luggage in a long time. What difference could an hour or so make? It would give her a chance to say a proper goodbye to lovely Xanthe. But there was no way Jake was going to change her mind about getting the 10am flight.

'Fine. I'll come to breakfast but that's it.'

'Lead the way,' said Jake and CJ walked ahead of him towards the suite, acutely aware of his gaze on her.

'Can you give me five minutes, let me grab a quick shower and look a bit more presentable? Jake said as they arrived. He gestured to his T-shirt and board shorts and CJ quickly looked away.

'Sure. Take as long as you like.'

If he picked up on her meaning he didn't let on, and headed towards another door. 'Make yourself at home, breakfast should be here any minute. I won't be long, but don't wait for us.'

CJ took a seat by the table. She'd left her phone behind on charge and regretted it, because as soon as she heard the sound of the water being turned on, all she could think of was Jake standing naked in the – no-doubt – luxurious shower. Why on earth did she still feel so drawn to a man who treated people so badly?

A knock signalled the welcome arrival of breakfast, which distracted her for a minute but as soon as the staff had gone her mind went into overload again. She could imagine Jake beneath the jets, the water streaming down those strong arms, his sculpted torso, then…

'Are you alright?'

CJ jumped, hands flying to her burning cheeks. She'd been so busy day-dreaming she'd not noticed the sound of the water stop. Jake was standing in front of her, fully clothed, hair still damp and she had a horrible feeling the thoughts she'd been having were written all over her face.

'I'm fine…err…absolutely.' She fixed her gaze firmly on the breakfast, lest she give anything more away.

'You sure? You don't look right.'

Oh for goodness' sake, why couldn't he drop the subject? Surely, he didn't actually think she was ill but knew exactly what had been on her mind and was now making her feel as awkward as possible? How irritating could he get?

'Honestly, I'm fine,' she said hotly, flashing him a defiant look.

'If you say so. Where's Xanthe got to? I'm starving.' He wandered off to his daughter's room and CJ quickly patted her cheeks to try to cool them. Soon they were back and she was glad of Xanthe's chatter.

They all sat down to breakfast and CJ immediately felt ravenous.

'Are you staying now, CJ?' Xanthe asked between mouthfuls of pancake, which was oozing with maple syrup.

CJ looked at Jake expectantly. He didn't have long to convince her to stay.

'CJ might still have to leave, Xanthe,' he said. 'But there is something on today and I think she might want to juggle her work around for it, if she can.'

Jake looked from one to the other, then pulled out his phone. 'Don't take too long over your breakfast, or we'll be late.'

'I s'pose while you're out I'm going with Brooke?' Xanthe's face fell.

'Not if you want to see the seals.'

Xanthe and CJ's heads snapped up. For a moment CJ wondered if she'd misheard. Xanthe obviously thought the same because she said, 'What do you mean, Daddy?'

Jake held the screen of his phone up for them. 'See? I've booked tickets for all of us to go on the seal-watching trip.'

Xanthe squealed and ran around the table to hug him. 'Really? Oh wow, I can't wait.'

Jake squeezed her back and then looked at CJ. 'I get if you need to go back instead. But we'd like you to join us, if you're free. And if you still want to go back home afterwards, I can ask my helicopter pilot to come and collect you at a time that's convenient.'

CJ took in his handsome face. She wanted to be angry with him but it was hard when his eyes were soft, imploring. Secretly, she was delighted he'd taken her advice on board to do something fun with Xanthe. 'Wouldn't you two rather go on your own?'

Xanthe moved from her dad to CJ and pulled gently on her arm. 'I really want you to be there too. Pppllleeaaasseee come with us.'

CJ felt herself torn — again.

'I can get a lift back to the mainland later?' She eyed Jake carefully.

'Absolutely. If you still want to head home, you can.'

If you still want to head home – he was sure of himself. As far as CJ was concerned, he was just postponing the inevitable. And the thought of seeing seals was tempting.

'OK, I will.'

Xanthe squealed again and danced around the room before sitting back up to finish her breakfast. CJ stole a glance at Jake and he shot her a hopeful smile.

It'll take more than that, she thought, as she went to get ready.

Lauren had planned to come round, so she dropped her a text to say she'd be later than planned. Within seconds her phone rang, but CJ ignored it and hurried to the rendezvous point.

The sun was climbing the sky, and out to sea a gentle swell heaved. CJ enjoyed the breeze on her face as she took in the gorgeous view to the harbour far below. She was so taken with it that she didn't hear father and daughter approach.

'Ready?' Jake asked and she spun around.

It was all she could do not to let her jaw drop open. He was wearing a black polo shirt, which accentuated his tan and showed off his powerful chest and biceps. The shirt was matched with a fresh set of board shorts which showed off his lovely legs.

'Don't you approve of what I'm wearing?' Amusement was written all over his face, as if he was well aware of her thoughts.

'Just worried you might catch your death, that's all,' she replied airily.

'Good to hear you're so concerned for my welfare. Glad I brought my jacket.' He nodded to the wall behind them, where a yachting jacket lay. 'Otherwise, will I pass? Or since you're meant to be finding me 'true love', should I let you go through my wardrobe as well?'

Despite his joke, CJ was shocked to realise it stung. The thought of having to help him find someone else to date, made her feel miserable. Although good luck to whoever ended up with him because they'd need it.

'What do you mean, finding you 'true love'?' asked Xanthe, looking from one to the other.

'Oh, it's nothing, don't worry,' Jake picked up his jacket and took his daughter's hand. 'CJ owns a dating agency and I thought maybe she could find someone for me, that was all. If you think that's a good idea and if she isn't too busy to keep me on her books.'

'But you've already got someone,' Xanthe said matter-of-factly and took CJ's hand too. 'Come on, let's go.'

CJ glanced at Jake, who was looking puzzled. What had Xanthe meant? Did she think her dad should stay true to his late wife? Or was there someone else on the scene CJ didn't know about? It wouldn't surprise her, particularly given the affair, and would explain why he never went on second dates. Though it didn't seem to fit; for all he was arrogant and infuriating, Jake didn't seem the type to be deceitful. Why lie, when you couldn't care less what people thought?

It was too exhausting to figure out. At least he'd acknowledged that he might not be her client for much longer, so it would soon be someone else's problem.

As they approached the harbour, CJ stopped in surprise. 'Are we going on the boat Xanthe and I saw here yesterday?'

It was the only one there.

'I think so, why?'

'Well, it's a public boat, I didn't think you'd want to…' She trailed off.

'Didn't want to, what?' Jake drawled, with a raised eyebrow.

'You know, you're well-known. I appreciate that makes it harder for you.'

'You're not suggesting I might be more of an attraction to people than the seals?' He was mocking her, but the fact was there was truth in it.

'Don't worry, I think the seals can hold their own,' she replied. 'I'm merely saying there will probably be lots of people on board and some are bound to recognise you. You could probably arrange your own private cruise.'

'Thank you for your concern, but I'm more than happy to join some fellow tourists for a few hours,' he replied airily. 'Besides, I was particularly drawn to this trip. So, shall we go?'

As the three of them made their way down the stone steps to the bobbing boat, CJ was deep in thought. Jake had specifically chosen this trip because she and Xanthe had seen it the day before. He seemed to have taken on board the need to spend more time with his daughter but if she wasn't mistaken, it was also his way of trying to make amends to her too. Was it dumb luck, or had he put some thought into what would be the right gesture? Either way it was working, and to her dismay her intention to leave the islands as soon as possible was starting to wane.

CHAPTER 16

There were audible gasps as Jake stepped aboard but he merely nodded and smiled at everyone. Within a few minutes the other day trippers had forgotten he was there, as the boat started on its way, the beauty of the Isles of Scilly enough to make them forget all about their famous companion.

It was no wonder it was designated an Area of Outstanding Natural Beauty and was unlike anywhere else CJ had been in the UK. The larger, occupied islands were surrounded by many smaller ones, coupled with outcrops of rock. The landscape changed at every turn, revealing more of its treasures to the visitors. CJ decided she would definitely book a trip for her mum and grandpa, they would love what the islands had to offer. Coming here would be just the tonic they needed, and something she'd be pleased to treat them to.

She turned her attention back to the trip. Each island boasted glorious white sand and aqua waters, making her feel that she was somewhere very exotic. The boat made its way to the Eastern Isles, favourite haunt of a population of Atlantic grey seals.

'Oh wow, look!' Xanthe exclaimed as she pointed to some sleek heads bobbing above the surface. The crew ensured there was a respectful distance to allow the visitors to witness the creatures, without disturbing them.

'Will we see any of the white fluffy ones?' Xanthe asked one of the crew.

'The pups, you mean? Unfortunately, you only see them in the autumn and the run-up to Christmas. They're all out at sea now and the young ones soon lose those white fluffy coats. Need to have a bit of waterproofing for all this weather, you see.'

Xanthe nodded seriously. 'That's OK, we can come back again in a few months' time, can't we Dad.'

It was more statement, than question.

Jake smiled. 'We'll see, but I agree, it'd certainly be great to come back and see the pups.'

CJ felt a sudden pang at the thought of the two of them returning to the islands without her, even though she was pleased to hear them making plans together.

Some of the seals were inquisitive and bobbed close to the boat, watching the visitors with their big eyes and long whiskers.

'This is incredible,' whispered CJ, who loved wildlife. 'They are so beautiful.'

'They certainly are,' Jake agreed.

CJ looked round to see him watching her and their eyes locked, his searching hers.

'I'm sorry about my awful behaviour,' he whispered, so as to not be overheard by Xanthe. 'Really sorry.'

'It's not the first time you've spoken out of turn.'

Jake had the good grace to look shame-faced. 'I know. You must think me some awful Hollywood type.' He hung his head. 'Hard to believe, but I'm actually not.'

'You're right. It is hard to believe.'

'Well, I hope you might agree to stay a little longer to let me convince you otherwise. Not least because I have you to thank for this.' He gestured around them and then to his daughter. 'You made me realise what was important.'

Xanthe sat back in her seat then, breaking their eye contact and Jake ruffled her hair affectionately, as she chatted away.

CJ watched the seals and took in the scenery with a big smile on her face. It was lovely to hear something from Jake that felt genuine. Half the time he seemed to be teasing her and the rest treating her like some sort of hired escort. She'd been furious with him but maybe he meant his apology? And she was delighted for Xanthe that they'd been able to prise him away from his business meetings and accounts for a few hours. Lost time with his child was something he could never buy back, for all his wealth, as CJ knew to her cost.

'Look CJ, look!' said Xanthe, tugging at her arm and pointing out another amazing sight. The pair was soon chattering away enthusiastically.

Jake sat back in his seat and watched them, two heads close together – one blonde like his, the other russet red. It was an amazing trip, expertly led and delivered, but the crew would have no idea how life-changing it was for him. This precious time out in nature, enjoying the beauty of the landscape and the islands' wildlife, alongside the daughter he loved so dearly, had made him realise a few home truths. This is what being a dad was all about, being present, doing things together. Not just sharing a space while one worked and the other watched films.

Jake thought of his mum who'd gently said as much to him over recent months. He'd not understood what she'd meant, had become defensive even. Although he'd arranged this boat trip to treat CJ and Xanthe, he'd got the most from it; far more than seeing seals and stunning views, lovely as that was. This trip was a turning point for him, one which he was determined to seize. First thing he'd do when they got back would be to tell his mum he finally understood. He could already picture the look of relief on her face.

This was probably one of the least expensive trips he'd paid for in forever and yet Jake would swap everything he owned for the value it had brought to his life. And he had CJ to thank for it. Now he was also desperate to persuade her to stay.

Sitting on the bench above the cliffs the previous afternoon, racking his brains as to what he could do to make amends, he'd remembered her questions about Xanthe and how the pair had discussed the seal trip. He'd hurried down to the ticket office and booked places on the boat, not expecting it to fix everything, but hoping it was a start. What he hadn't imagined was the impact it would have on his own life.

As if reading his thoughts, CJ turned to him with a big broad smile, before she was distracted once again by Xanthe.

Jake drank her in. There seemed to be magic in the air around these Eastern Isles and he didn't want it to end. He leaned in closer to them and his gaze followed his daughter's finger as she pointed out something else. And just for a moment, Jake allowed all his troubles to float away on the tide.

CHAPTER 17

All too soon they were back on the quay at St Mary's, with Jake saying goodbye to their star-struck, fellow passengers. CJ watched the charming way he spared a few words or a joke with each person in turn, and recognised the glow reflected in their faces. She knew what it was like to have the former movie star's full attention. It was mesmerising, like having the sun shine just on you.

She and Xanthe stood waiting and despite the lovely trip, CJ was sad that it was over. Finally, the last of the visitors departed. Jake shook hands with the crew, before climbing the steps to join them on the harbour. He clapped his hands.

'Right then ladies, time for lunch. Where would you like to go?'

Both Xanthe and CJ's jaws dropped open.

He looked from one face to the other and laughed. 'Hey, you can't blame a guy for wanting to treat you two, can you? So come on, where's it to be?'

'Oh, I know, I know,' cried Xanthe. She seemed delighted that Jake was going to be spending more time with them. 'The café, where we had the drinks, CJ. The one by the pretty beach.'

'Porthcressa,' CJ said softly.

'That's it. Can we go there?' Xanthe asked.

Jake raised a quizzical eyebrow to CJ as if seeking confirmation that the venue was suitable.

'It is a lovely spot,' CJ affirmed. 'Though perhaps not quite what you had in mind.'

'How so?'

'Well, it's a pretty café by the beach. Not a five-star restaurant.'

'I can slum it for one meal,' Jake said breaking into a grin. 'This may come as a shock but I don't spend all my time eating at top restaurants; I actually prefer things simpler. It's just my business often dictates what venues I go to.'

'So can we go to the cafe?' Xanthe was looking from one to the other.

'We certainly can,' said Jake. 'Assuming you have the time, CJ? I appreciate you were planning to head back to the mainland, so we'd understand if you can't join us.'

She could feel his gaze on her, as if trying to gauge her reaction. Bottom line was, she was having a good time and didn't want it to end. 'No, it's fine, I can spare some more time. I'd love to come to lunch.'

Satisfied, Xanthe skipped ahead as they made their way through the main street of St Mary's, with its array of attractive shops.

Jake touched CJ's arm to catch her attention. 'Once again I'm sorry about yesterday. I behaved very badly. It was something else which had upset me but I took out my bad mood on you and had no right to. I hope today is a start towards making it up to you.'

CJ was surprised by his sincerity. It was at odds with the man who'd made her come to the islands in the first place, and who thought nothing of cheating on his wife. Which was the real Jake?

'You're right about your behaviour and whatever you had going on wasn't my fault,' she said carefully. 'But let's draw a line under it and enjoy the day.'

He nodded and they continued along the street, following in Xanthe's footsteps. Every now and then CJ noticed other people doing a double-take as they spotted the famous star, or could hear his name whispered by passers-by. She wasn't sure if he noticed or not.

'I can't remember when I last did this,' he said.

'Did what?'

'Did nothing. Had some time off. Went on a boat trip that wasn't for work. As for strolling through a nice town, heading to a 'pretty' café for lunch, not for a long, long time. It hasn't always been possible, or practical. I've missed it.'

He stopped and turned to her, his face earnest. 'And it's thanks to you, CJ. I've spent a lot of time with Xanthe since… well, over the past couple of years,' he faltered. 'But most of that has been her hanging around while I head to business meetings and the like. Those three hours on the water were a light bulb moment for me.'

'Really?'

'Yes.' His voice was thick with emotion. 'I realised I'm missing out on Xanthe. She's growing up fast and I want to have precious memories with her to look back on.'

CJ was stunned to hear his voice crack with emotion. She reached out and squeezed his hand, trying to ignore the electricity shooting through her as they touched. 'There's still time,' she said softly. 'And today is a good start.'

'You're right.' He smiled. 'Today is a very good start. In lots of ways.'

He held her gaze before Xanthe called out, urging them to hurry up. Jake let go of her hand and jogged to catch up with his daughter.

CJ felt like punching the air. Maybe things were going to change for the Mastersons from now on.

But what did he mean by today being a good start in 'lots of ways'? She felt he wasn't wholly talking about Xanthe, but couldn't be sure. With dismay she realised there was one thing she was certain of; the more time she spent with Jake, the stronger her feelings for him. That would surely spell disaster? Even if she decided to stay, CJ only had a few short days before Jake would be out of her life, their future contact reduced to details of his next date with one of her clients. Worse, she realised it wasn't just Jake she would miss, as Xanthe hurried her along to the café.

CHAPTER 18

Lunch was delicious. CJ tucked into a salad bursting with fresh figs and Cornish goat's cheese. Jake had chosen a seafood platter, making the most of the local catch. For a treat, Xanthe was allowed to have burger and fries and she chattered away, between mouthfuls.

'Did you see that young seal who seemed to be looking at us all the time? The one on the far side. He was gorgeous. Dad, can we have one for a pet?'

Jake, who was drinking some cold beer, spluttered with shock, causing CJ and Xanthe to burst out laughing. 'I don't think so,' he said when he'd recovered. 'Firstly, they are wild animals and need to live in their own habitat. It's fine to go with experts to see them but otherwise we need to leave them be, not take one home and pop it in the swimming pool.'

'I know,' said Xanthe. 'But they are sooooooooo cute.'

'Well, that was my other point,' continued her father. 'They look cute when they're in their home environment, but I'm sure they wouldn't look that way if they were hulking around the house.'

They all laughed again.

'They were lovely though, weren't they,' CJ said dreamily.

'They certainly were, particularly with those beautiful, big eyes,' Jake murmured and she realised he was staring straight at her.

'But still too big to be a pet,' chirped Xanthe, totally oblivious.

'Absolutely.' Jake tore his gaze away from CJ and watched his daughter dunk a couple of fries into her sauce.

'So, in that case can we get a puppy instead? Or a kitten?'

'Oh my, I've walked straight into a trap.'

CJ couldn't help but chuckle, Xanthe had certainly pulled a number on her father.

'Not exactly a trap, but I've been thinking about it a lot, Dad. If I had a puppy then you wouldn't have to worry about me so much when you had to work.'

Jake put his knife and fork down and eyed his daughter seriously. 'A few things are going to start changing around here, Xanthe. I want us to do more things together and even when we can't go on trips, I'd like to hang out with you more. If that's OK with you?'

Xanthe beamed. 'That would be great.'

'Good. A deal then.' Jake bumped fists with her and then picked up his cutlery.

'But a dog would be good for you too, Daddy. It could go out on runs with you.'

'Wow, you've got it all worked out, haven't you.'

They laughed at Xanthe's ingenuity, though CJ couldn't help feel a pang of envy. She wondered if they would get a dog and what adventures they'd go on together. She was as enchanted by Xanthe as she was by her father, and the thought of not spending time with them after this week was agonising. It felt like she was alighting from a train as it continued on its onward journey without her.

Xanthe was making the most of being spoilt by her father and was allowed another ice cream after lunch. They watched her go to the counter to order it.

'Your business is impressive, I've been reading up on it,' Jake said out of the blue.

CJ swelled with pride. This coming from a successful entrepreneur!

'How did it start?'

'I studied psychology at university and people always interested me. Then one might my flatmate was bemoaning the fact that she couldn't find a decent boyfriend and I said, 'have you considered Chris?' He was one of our friends and she'd never thought of him in that way before. They'll be celebrating their fifth wedding anniversary next month.' CJ dug her fork into some salad leaves. 'A couple of other friends heard about it and I found someone for each of them too. Then I realised I had a way of approaching it, developed my idea and ran it alongside my first job. It took off, so, I quit my job and set up the business.'

'Well, it's certainly successful. But has your formula not worked for you?'

CJ shuddered as that horrible night last year came to mind. She could still feel her happiness as she'd headed to Angus's flat to surprise him, followed by the confusion and despair as his semi-naked work colleague wandered out from his bedroom. She pushed the memory away. 'No,' she answered as calmly as she could. 'Not for me. I think it's like a lot of things in life, you can make it work for others but not so easily for yourself. Besides the business takes up most of my time.'

'Well, I know what that's like. But what is....

Whatever Jake wanted to know had to wait, because CJ's phone rang.

'I'm sorry, I should get this. It's my mum, and my grandpa's not been too well recently.'

'Sure, of course.'

Fortunately, CJ's mum was letting her know all was well and their brief conversation ended as Xanthe returned to the table, carrying a bowl full of strawberry ice cream.

'That looks pretty good,' Jake said as she dug her spoon in. Then he turned to CJ. 'Everything OK?'

'All fine. Grandpa was seriously ill recently but he's doing OK now. Mum's just been up to see him, so was giving me an update.'

Jake gave a nod of understanding. Had he remembered what she'd said on their first night here about other people having worries too? A lot had happened since.

'Is it just your mum and grandpa?'

'No, I've got a younger brother too – Tim. He's a lawyer. Oh, and my dad, though I don't see much of him. He and my mum split up when I was quite small and he moved away. We speak a bit but...well you know how it is. When he left, Grandpa stepped into his role, so we're pretty close.'

Now perhaps Jake would realise why she was so keen that his and Xanthe's relationship should be rock solid. He certainly seemed be listening intently, his chin resting on his hand.

'Grandpa would love it here though,' CJ gestured around them. 'And wait 'til I tell him I've been in a helicopter. He's going to be so jealous.'

'He's never been in one?'

'No. I know it's something he'd love to do, so I must arrange it for him, now he's on the mend. Oh Xanthe, you've got ice cream all over your face!'

The conversation turned to the dessert antics and afterwards they headed to the water's edge. The tide at Porthcressa was heading out, pulling gently against the silky sand as it retreated. There was warmth in the spring sunshine. Xanthe was examining a shell she'd found.

'Hard to believe there's a nasty squall rolling,' said Jake, staring out to the horizon.

'Really?'

'That's what's forecast for tomorrow afternoon. I expect this place will look completely different then. It seems impossible, when today is so glorious. I can understand why Sam and Tara call this place home for much of the year.'

'Thank you,' said CJ.

He turned, a puzzled look on his face. 'For what?'

'For bringing me here.'

Jake laughed, a smile spreading across his face. 'You weren't too keen as I recall. And considering the way I've behaved I'd have thought you couldn't wait to leave. Glad you've changed your mind.'

'Oh, I haven't changed my mind about all that,' responded CJ, tilting her chin. 'I still don't see why you needed me to come with you, and you have been a real pain.'

He held her gaze. 'And yet despite it all, it's worked out rather well, don't you think?'

Why did Jake Masterson have to be so damn dazzling? She needed to play things cool. 'It depends. I mean, if I get you a successful date out of it, then it will have been worth it.'

Jake unexpectedly caught her by the waist, pulling her in close to him. 'Don't tease me, CJ.' His voice was hoarse.

'Tease you? I'm not teasing you.'

'You are - don't you realise what you do to me?'

He felt it too, he wasn't immune?

CJ's heart was hammering in her chest. 'I…I…don't think this is a good idea. It makes things too complicated.'

'It's not a question of complicated, it's a matter of desire.'

His mouth was millimetres from hers. If she moved a tiny step, they would be able to claim each other. And yet…a voice in her head was urging caution. Getting involved with him was only going to lead to torment. Jake still seemed hung up on his wife. She'd been sensational and yet he'd still cheated on her. What hope did CJ have?

Aware of the danger her emotions were in, CJ pushed him away, ignoring his hurt look. Whatever it was he wanted from her, she had to resist because she wasn't sure she would be able to recover from Jake Masterson's charms.

CHAPTER 19

Conscious Jake was watching her intently, CJ decided her best ally was his daughter. 'You know what, I think it's warm enough for another paddle. How about it Xanthe?' she called brightly.

Xanthe came bounding over.

'I thought we could get your dad to sample the water.'

'Yeah.'

'I don't know,' protested Jake, his face now a mask. 'It seems pretty cold.'

'We went in the other day, didn't we Xanthe. But you know, if you can't handle it…if you're not as tough as us girls…' CJ and Xanthe folded their arms and looked challengingly at Jake.

'Well, if you put it like that, I can go one better,' he said, pulling off his leather deck shoes.

Then to CJ's astonishment he tore off his polo shirt, revealing his strong chest. She could see the muscles rippling beneath the surface. She swallowed hard. Jake turned and ran into the water, seeming to not mind the cold. After a few feet, he dived beneath the waves, ripples spreading in his wake.

For what seemed like an age he didn't reappear and CJ started to feel anxious. She glanced at Xanthe who didn't seem at all concerned. Finally, he surfaced, blond hair turned dark by the water. He turned, wiping the water from his face, before giving them a cheery wave.

'Come on in, it's lovely.'

'No way. We're not falling for that trick,' CJ called. She turned to Xanthe. 'We could paddle though.'

The pair quickly took off their shoes and once again dipped their toes into the blue waters.

Jake seemed at home, cutting through the water with ease. CJ wondered if he did much swimming and was struck by how little she knew about him. Though from what she'd seen of his firm body it was evident he worked out regularly. That moment when he'd torn off his shirt…the heat and fire of desire had raged through her whole body, causing her to shudder even now.

'Are you still cold?' asked Xanthe.

'A little.'

It wasn't a total white lie because the Atlantic waters had yet to warm up fully after winter.

Xanthe found a small crab at the edge of the waves and the pair watched it as it made its way back out to sea, their blonde and titian heads pressed closely together. They were so absorbed they didn't notice Jake, who'd swum to the right of the beach, then tiptoed across the sands, heading towards them from behind. Suddenly, he grabbed them both into a wet hug.

'Gotcha!' he shouted and they both screamed.

An older couple, sitting at the top of the beach, looked up to see what the commotion was.

'We're soaked!' exclaimed Xanthe and she turned and kicked a spray of water all over him.

Laughing, CJ joined in.

'Big mistake, ladies. Massive,' warned Jake, tearing through the fountain of water they were making.

Xanthe shrieked and ran away, heading towards the rocks at the far side of the beach.

He ran after her, the water dripping from his body. In a few short strides he was alongside her, pulling her into a big bear hug, trapping her arms while she squealed with excitement and delight.

'Fee, fie, fo, fum,' he said nuzzling his daughter's neck. Then as easily as if she were made of feathers, he pulled her up over his shoulder and strode out into the water, Xanthe laughing and shouting, whilst trying unsuccessfully to escape.

'Daddy, no!'

To no avail. Quick as a flash, Jake tossed her – gently – into the sea.

She bobbed up again a few seconds later and he put his hand out to help her. She stood in soaking wet clothes, laughing and trying to pull him into the water. CJ, who was still on the shoreline couldn't stop laughing too.

'I can't believe you did that.' Xanthe cried though she was obviously chuffed to be having so much fun with her dad. CJ wondered when was the last time they'd done something like this together – if ever. Xanthe dipped back into the water and swam parallel to the beach for a minute or two.

'You see, I told you it was great once you get in,' said Jake, walking along beside her.

Then Xanthe jumped up and beckoned to her dad. He bent down and she whispered something into his ear. They both looked at CJ and started to walk towards her through the waves. The penny dropped.

'Oh no you don't!' cried CJ and she started to run away. Although she hiked and ran regularly, it was tougher running uphill through sand. Even so, she'd gone quite a way by the time Jake caught her. He pulled her down onto the beach, deftly landing beneath her so as to break her fall. She could feel the hardness of his wet body beneath hers and she found herself reaching out to touch the smooth firm skin of his chest and shoulder.

Jake groaned and entwined his fingers in her copper hair, pulling her towards him. His mouth found hers, softly at first, then more urgently. As their kiss deepened, she found her own desire growing, meeting his, forgetting all about this island and the beach and…

'I thought you were going to catch her?'

Xanthe's voice snapped them back to reality and they pulled apart quickly, though Jake didn't loosen his grip. Her face came into view.

'I have done, as ordered.' Jake smiled up at his daughter.

'Have you sold me out?' CJ looked from one to the other.

'Sort of,' Xanthe said. 'Though Dad did say he would drop you in the water too.'

'And that's precisely what I'm going to do,' announced Jake.

In a flash he sprung up from the sand, still holding CJ fast. Then, as she struggled to get free, he slung her over his shoulder almost as easily as he had his daughter, and she found herself staring down his smooth brown back to his cute butt. She continued to struggle but without using her full strength, softly beating her fists against his bare back and trying hard not to think what it would be like to run her fingertips over it.

'Let me go!' she laughed, the prospect of being dropped in the cool waters not filling her with much enthusiasm.

'Say please.'

'No way.'

Jake spun around to talk to Xanthe, without loosening his grip, giving CJ a sudden view of the sea. 'What do you think, m'hearty? Do you think the prisoner deserves mercy?'

'No!' shouted Xanthe.

'Oh well, sorry CJ, the boss has spoken.'

CJ felt him shrug and he turned and continued towards the water.

'I won't forget this, Xanthe,' laughed CJ.

Even so, she was still surprised when Jake really did start to walk into the waves and so decided to make one last ditch attempt at escape. She was a strong woman and as she wriggled and fought, she was pleased that Jake was finding it hard to keep hold of her, so much so that when he was waist deep, he let go and she plunged into the water. She gasped as the cold hit but Jake was right, after a few moments it wasn't so bad. CJ surfaced, wiping the water from her face, her red hair slick down her back.

She stood before him, clothes clinging to her body. Her pink shirt had gone almost see-through, revealing the lacy underwear beneath. This time there was no doubting the look on his face, it was one of naked desire and she felt the same way.

'CJ,' he groaned. 'What are you doing to me? I can't stand much more of this, I need…I want…' The words were wrenched from his throat.

CJ said nothing but remained still, not daring to step forward in case she was lost, enveloped by his passion and her own.

'Dad, what are you doing? You're not meant to let her get away.' Xanthe's voice broke the spell once again.

CJ plastered a smile onto her face. 'I think you should change sides, Xanthe. We girls always get the upper hand.' Quick as a flash she dived at Jake, rugby tackling him. He hadn't been expecting it and they both fell back into the water with a splash.

As they surfaced again Jake was spluttering. 'I see I'm going to have to be careful. I've seen a new side to you.'

'Yeah, well, don't dish it out if you can't take it.' CJ clapped her hands, satisfied her revenge was complete.

'That was great,' said Xanthe, admiringly. 'Can we get him again?'

'Why not? It's not as if we have to worry about getting our clothes wet.'

For the next half hour they chased Jake around the water. Sometimes he allowed himself to be dunked by the pair, other times he turned and splashed them, or grabbed them, before sending them flying into the gentle waves again. Their cries and laughter echoed around the cove.

Eventually, tired out, they decided to head back.

'You know we have to drip all the way back to the hotel in our wet clothes now?' said CJ.

'Ah well, I have a plan. You two will be freezing if we walk. I'm going to call Brooke and see if someone can come and get us in that battered old Land Rover they use. I wouldn't want them to bring their usual car, we'll ruin the seats.'

CJ was touched by his consideration; it would be easy to exploit his wealth and power and assume the hotel would sort out some soaked upholstery.

They were still chatting and joking together as they made their way out of the water, towards their jackets and shoes.

Suddenly Jake stopped dead in his tracks and his whole body stiffened.

CJ followed his gaze to a man standing beside their belongings, waiting. The look on his face was as cool as the waters they'd just been playing in. He was tall and quite handsome, with light brown hair and eyes, but wasn't as broad as Jake. He would have been better looking, were it not for the look of disdain on his face. Xanthe noticed him and ran across the sands.

'Derrick, you're here,' she shouted.

She went to give him a hug but he put his hand out to stop her. 'Don't, Xanthe,' he said. 'You're soaking wet and late for your lessons. I had to come looking for you.'

Xanthe's face fell. The message was clear; this stranger did not approve. CJ felt Jake tense beside her. This new person's arrival had changed the atmosphere completely and she shivered.

The movement drew the man's attention to her and slowly he checked out her body, his stare lingering on her wet shirt. Unlike the way Jake had looked at her, it gave her the creeps and instinctively she crossed her arms over her body.

The man gave her a twisted smile. 'I'm Derrick, Xanthe's tutor. Who are you?'

CHAPTER 20

The silvery moon was nearly full and coupled with the sweep of the Bishop Rock lighthouse, it pierced the darkness of the night sky.

Jake was glad of the anonymity the evening afforded him, as he stood on the cliff path staring out to sea, watching the light dancing on the waves far below. Behind him was the warm orange glow from the hotel and he was conscious that both Xanthe and CJ were there, relaxing and untroubled.

Derrick had messaged him to say he'd be arriving today but his appearance on the beach and obvious disapproval had stunned him. True, he was flirting with CJ – what man in their right mind wouldn't be? Besides, she'd completely changed his life by helping to show him the error of his ways where Xanthe was concerned. The barriers between him and his daughter had been there way before her mother's death. When he gave himself a moment to consider such things – which was rare – Jake knew the fault was his. It was always one more business meeting, one more set of accounts to pore over, at the expense of his beloved child. Never a deliberate act but a habit that had gone unnoticed – until now.

Now Derrick had come along and with one look made his time with CJ seem wrong. But surely it wasn't?

He cursed himself for even caring what Derrick thought and allowing him to get under his skin, again. Within a few seconds he'd made Jake feel bad about the fun time he was having with a new woman in his life.

And what of CJ?

She was an unexpected surprise. Of course he'd fancied her from the moment he'd seen her photo on her website, but it was her personality he was so taken with. He loved how she embraced life, her compassion for Xanthe and her own family, and above all the way she stood up to him. CJ was both fascinating and terrifying in equal measure. Now Derrick, of all people, had made it feel sullied. Jake wished he'd never asked him to come. Far better that it had just been the three of them.

The three of them.

He stopped for a moment. Could that be something?

Should it be?

'No, it's too risky,' he cursed aloud, balling his hands into fists and pacing the path. It had endured far worse erosion through countless centuries of wind, rain and sea spray – more than one troubled soul could do.

Jake heard footsteps. The lightness of step sounded like CJ and he turned to see her approaching, her red hair catching the faint light and creating a halo around her.

'Beautiful evening,' she said.

After all that had happened between them, it had come to this? Talking about the weather?

'It is.' His voice was soft and low and he turned back to look at the night sky. Clouds were passing overhead, allowing glimpses of the thousands of stars twinkling far above. At any other time it would be truly magical.

'Do you mind me joining you? I mean, if you'd rather be alone I can go back to my room?'

'Not sure I'm much company, but you're welcome to stay,' he said without turning around.

They fell into an uneasy silence, listening to the rise and fall of the sea. They had both gone through plenty of emotions since their first meeting; annoyance, anger, desire but never awkwardness. It hung heavily between them now.

Jake wondered if he should explain what was troubling him but couldn't find the words. It annoyed him that Derrick's arrival made him question his feelings for CJ, but it had and now he was holding her at arm's length. Keep it simple, that was the plan. 'Did you get your clothes dried?'

'Yep. The concierge sorted it.'

'And you didn't get too cold? You seemed to be shivering by the time we got back.'

'No, I was fine. I took a shower, had a cup of tea, that sort of thing.'

For a second, a thought of CJ in the shower flashed through his mind but he quickly stamped on it.

'Is it a business dinner tomorrow?'

He glanced at her. This morning CJ had planned to leave the islands, was she now happy to stay? Jake realised that the events of the afternoon meant he'd forgotten to ask. She gave him a faint smile.

'They've moved it to lunchtime,' he said. 'Douglas and Barbara and some of the others need to get back and the weather's drawing in. If that's OK?'

She nodded and he physically relaxed.

'I liked Douglas and Barbara a lot, they were very welcoming.' Her voice was soft and low. 'They were kind enough to ask about my dating agency.'

'You made quite an impression on them too, by all accounts.'

'Good to hear. They thought…' she started, then stopped.

He sighed. 'I know what they thought. Don't worry, I've explained everything. That we have a business arrangement for the week and there's nothing more to our relationship.'

The air stilled. Without needing to look, he could tell his words had hurt her. Was this the right thing to do, to push away the woman who had brought joy back into his life? He shook the thought away.

Of course it was.

He had to protect himself from the misery and chaos that he'd only recently recovered from. And there was a need to protect CJ too. He was damaged goods and it wasn't fair to lead her on.

'Good, I'm glad Douglas and Barbara understand.' CJ's voice was flat and impassive. 'They're a nice couple and I wouldn't want them to have the wrong idea.'

He stole another sideways glance at her. She looked so beautiful, the moonlight on her ivory skin, the sexy red dress she'd worn to dinner, rippling in the breeze. How he wanted to take her in his arms, feel the warmth of her body against his, hold her and be held by her. He turned away quickly, his back a solid wall between them. Despite this, she filled his senses. There was a faint waft of her perfume on the evening breeze and he was acutely aware of every movement she made, as if she was a part of his very being. He heard her give the faintest of sighs.

'Look, it's getting late. I'd best get some sleep.'

'OK.' He was gutted but refused to turn around. Didn't trust himself.

'See you at breakfast?'

'No, I have an early start. I'll collect you at twelve-thirty.'

'Fine. See you then.'

He listened to her footsteps as she started to walk away. Then a thought crossed his mind and he called out. 'CJ.'

She spun around, a look of hope on her face.

'I wanted to thank you again for your help with Xanthe. I'd forgotten…' Jake couldn't express what he was feeling.

She stood still, waiting for him to finish, but he offered nothing more. A beam from the lighthouse swept across them.

'Well, goodnight.'

He watched her head towards the warm glow of the hotel.

When she was out of sight, Jake swore faintly. Deep down he'd wanted to reach out, bury his face in her soft hair, feel her closeness – but that was dangerous. What a day. On the boat and beach he'd started to allow this feisty, amazing woman into his life, but the look on Derrick's face had reminded Jake of the misery he'd endured. Since his wife's death, only one person had the key to his heart, Xanthe. Best to keep it that way.

CJ might wonder why things had changed but it wasn't fair to string her along. He didn't want to be a client of her dating agency any more either, though he'd give her a glowing review.

No, it was better this way, focussing solely on his daughter and work.

Even so, Jake was surprised by the wretched sense of loss. He pushed it into a deep recess of his mind; emotions led to dark places. Places he couldn't afford to go.

CHAPTER 21

CJ made herself a comforting hot chocolate when she returned to the room. She'd vowed not to look out again across the cliff top to see if she could spot Jake, yet did so instinctively. He was still where she'd left him. She drew the curtains sharply and retreated to the sofa.

There was only one reason she could think of for this sudden change and it was the one she dreaded; Jake was still in love with his late wife. Seeing Derrick who'd been with the family a long time had no doubt made him feel guilty about laughing and messing around with her on the beach.

CJ opened her laptop and typed 'Jake Masterson wife' into the search engine. Melissa. Of course, that had been her name. CJ had seen her photo before and each time she was stunned by her beauty. She read on.

They'd met at a drama summer school in the US. From there he got a contract as a model, which was hardly surprising. Movies soon followed. Melissa picked up acting parts too, though his success rapidly overtook hers. What would that do to a relationship, if you both started in the same industry and one eclipsed the other?

CJ scrolled on and came across a wedding photo. It was strange to see a much younger Jake, barely out of his teens. He and Melissa were standing with their arms draped around each other. The bride was wearing a cream lace mini-dress, with knee high white boots. She was holding a single red rose, with a matching ribbon holding her long dark hair in a ponytail. Her blue eyes, identical to Xanthe's – still shone out from the image. Jake was wearing cream chinos and a white shirt. He was smiling happily at the camera. There seemed to be no sign of the guarded look which haunted him now, instead he looked untroubled and hopeful.

Young film stars reveal their secret Vegas wedding! declared the headline.

They eloped? Wow, what did that mean?

Jake Masterson seemed too in control of his life to do something crazy like run away to get wed. In CJ's experience there were usually two reasons for people to run off to get married in secret. The first was that they were madly in love and couldn't wait any longer to tie the knot, particularly if they didn't want to wait for elaborate arrangements. The other was when one, or both, families weren't keen on the match. Which was it in this case? They certainly looked happy so perhaps as new film stars, they wanted something small and private.

Whatever the reason, it wasn't something she could ask Jake. Especially now there was an emotional gulf between them.

CJ continued. There were lots of images of the couple in the early days of their marriage, on the red carpet at the Oscars, snapped shopping in LA or London, on holiday in exotic locations. There were articles in various magazines – about film roles, their life together, their future dreams.

Next was an interview with Jake when Xanthe was born, with a few carefully taken photos of the new baby. CJ smiled at how lovingly he spoke about his new daughter. Whatever was now going on between Jake and her, she hoped he'd been serious when he described having a light bulb moment about how he prioritised his time. Perhaps that explained why he'd cooled towards CJ? Jake should always put Xanthe's needs first and it was great they seemed to be reconnecting but surely that didn't preclude romance in his life too?

There was a flurry of articles about the young family and then nothing. Occasional shots snapped by the paparazzi, but no interviews or photo shoots. Even when Jake unveiled a new start-up company, there was merely a press statement, plus a couple of articles which stuck strictly to business. No mention of his personal life.

The psychologist in CJ was intrigued. Did they decide they wanted more privacy after Xanthe was born? Or did something happen? Was it to do with the affair? She couldn't imagine what it was like to be splashed all over the newspapers and snapped by photographers whilst popping out for milk. The press would be quick to publicise any sort of scandal, so perhaps that was why they kept out of the public eye?

Deep in thought, she sipped the remainder of her hot chocolate, then turned her attention back to her laptop.

News of Melissa's death came next. She gasped when she saw some intrusive long-lens shots taken at the funeral, which showed a pale and drawn Jake, standing by the graveside, holding a young Xanthe's hand. They each held a red rose, its colour stark against the black clothing of the gathered mourners. CJ's mind jumped back to the wedding photo of Melissa holding a similar rose and a tear rolled down her cheek. It must have been awful for Jake and Xanthe and even worse being in the spotlight with the photos splashed all over the world.

According to the reports, Melissa had gone out on her favourite horse but later the steed had returned, minus its rider. A search party led by Jake ensued, and they found her body soon afterwards. The coroner's verdict was accidental death.

CJ quietly closed the laptop. That was a little over three years ago. CJ realised how lucky she'd been not to have suffered grief in her life. She couldn't imagine what it must be like to lose the person you thought you'd grow old with.

It was hardly surprising Jake was mixed up, sometimes getting close to her, then putting space between them. Understandable, but still sheer agony because she'd allowed him into her heart.

But there were just another couple of days to go and then the trip would be over. CJ would go back to her life and after time would forget all about Jake.

You've got to be kidding.

The pain of losing him was going to last a long time. Sadness weighed on her as she rinsed out her mug, then pulled the curtain back and looked towards the cliffs. Jake was no longer there.

CHAPTER 22

A breeze had picked up overnight. CJ took an early morning swim in the hotel pool, allowing the exercise to calm her troubled thoughts. Afterwards she had a late breakfast on her own in the pretty breakfast room; the hubbub from the other guests a welcome distraction.

Then it was back to her room to deal with her business emails. Thankfully there were lots of them and they needed her full attention. As soon as she got home she would place the job advert for an assistant.

CJ was proud of the method she'd developed to match couples but it took a lot of concentration, which was what she needed today. As well as the questionnaire and interview, she would also carefully study the photos they'd submitted.

'What are you telling me?' she'd ask each photo in turn, taking note of details such as the clothes the client was wearing and the background. Some would send in happy holiday pictures, others more formal shots in a professional environment. The snaps they had chosen to send was another piece of the puzzle.

CJ was determined not to lose the personal touch and an assistant would allow her the time to do just that. Even so, it would be great to share her skills with someone else so they could answer more of the requests made by prospective clients.

At noon she stopped and went to choose something to wear, opting for a deep green, calf-length wool dress. Her mum, whose colouring she'd inherited, always drummed into her the need to celebrate her Irish roots and this outfit certainly did that.

CJ was carefully applying the finishing touches to her make-up when there was a knock at the door. She glanced at her phone – it was 12.20pm. She hurried to the door.

'You're early,' she declared, swinging it wide open.

Derrick was standing there and without asking for an invitation, stepped over the threshold. Not for the first time, CJ felt uncomfortable.

'Can I do something for you?' she asked. 'Is Xanthe OK?'

'Xanthe's fine. Xanthe's always fine.' He waved a hand dismissively as he took in the room.

For a tutor who taught a billionaire's daughter, he was badly turned out, with half his shirt undone and the rest hanging out of his trousers. It was weird. He walked up to the French windows and looked out over the garden.

'Nice,' he said. 'Not a bad situation for an escort.'

CJ gasped. It was pretty clear what Derrick was inferring. She felt the heat rise in her cheeks. 'It's purely a professional arrangement,' she said firmly, following him.

'I'm sure it is.' Derrick continued to take in the view.

When he turned, she realised he could have been good-looking, but for the fact his personality showed on his face. He seemed to sport a slight sneer at all times. It was clear he looked down on everyone and everything, with a touch of nastiness thrown in for good measure.

'I hope it is merely a 'professional' arrangement for your sake, CJ.'

'What's my relationship with Jake, or anyone else got to do with you?'

'Oh, believe me, it's nothing to do with me, though a pretty woman like you…' His gaze swept her body and once again she crossed her arms, glad she'd left the door ajar. 'A pretty woman like you is no doubt a magnet for someone like him. And I can see why you'd be attracted to the billionaire Jake Masterson.'

CJ felt anger rise. How dare he emphasise the word billionaire, as if that was why she was here! She was tempted to tell him that Jake had more or less forced her to come to the islands, but a sixth sense told her it wouldn't be a good idea. So she held her tongue, though she was bristling with rage.

'Take it from me, he isn't all he seems, all charm and easy manners,' said Derrick. 'I've been a part of the family for a long time and I'm well aware of what really went on behind the scenes. Believe me, Jake Masterson isn't a nice man and you'd do well to steer clear of him.'

CJ remembered Tara's words about the affair but she wasn't going to let on what she'd been told. 'Thanks for the warning, I'll bear it in mind.'

She was tempted to add there was nothing going on between her and Jake – nor would there likely ever be, but she'd be damned if she'd give Derrick the satisfaction of knowing that either.

He studied her for a moment, gave a brief nod, then walked towards the door, tracing a finger slowly along the dressing table as he did so. Then he paused, looking into the full-length mirror, and ruffled his hands through his hair until it looked unkempt and untidy. CJ watched him with astonishment.

'The impact of Melissa's death on Jake was huge, but then, she was an incredible woman. A one off. Irreplaceable.' Derrick was still looking at himself.

CJ knew he was sticking the knife in but it played on her worst fears, of wondering how she could ever match the glamorous, late Mrs Masterson.

'I'm afraid Jake's attitude towards women is the same as it is for most things, a transaction. Something to be bought, used and then discarded, when something better comes along.'

So, it would seem Derrick had known about Jake's affair? Given he seemed to be full of admiration for Melissa, it would explain why there was palpable tension between the two men.

They were standing near the doorway now and CJ was desperate to get rid of him. Playing along might do the trick. 'I appreciate you coming to tell me all this.' She spoke more pleasantly than she felt. 'But there's no need.'

She reached around him and opened the door wider, hoping he'd take the hint. 'I can assure you I have absolutely no interest in Jake. My accompanying him here is merely a business arrangement and a reluctant one at that. I don't particularly warm to the guy and when this week is up, I've no desire to ever see him again.'

Without warning, Derrick reached out and caught his hand into the back of her hair, burrowing his fingers in deep and firmly, yanking her sharply towards him. Before she had time to react, his hard, thin lips were pressing against hers. CJ was so stunned that it took a second or two to realise what was happening. As she was about to fight back, she heard a loud cough and Derrick immediately let her go.

'Oh, sorry are we late? CJ and I have been getting to know each other better and…well you know how it is, we sort of lost track of time,' Derrick said smoothly, a false grin on his face.

Standing in the doorway, face like thunder, was Jake.

To her horror, CJ realised how it looked. When Jake arrived the door was half open, and to all intents and purposes, it looked like she and Derrick were embroiled in a passionate embrace. Add to that Derrick's words, and it gave the impression they'd spent the morning tumbling together between the sheets. 'No, it isn't how it seems Jake…it was Derrick, he…' she blurted out quickly.

'Don't explain.' Jake cut her off coldly. 'As you said yourself, ours is merely a business arrangement and a reluctant one at that. What you get up to in your free time is up to you.'

CJ's hands flew to her mouth. Not only had Jake found the pair of them seemingly in some kind of tryst but he'd also heard the last thing she'd said – words used in an attempt to get rid of Derrick. Jake was looking Derrick up and down and CJ realised he was taking in the other man's ruffled hair and half undone shirt. Could it look any more damning? The penny dropped. 'No, this is a set-up. Please Jake, I was just…'

'Don't embarrass yourself CJ.' His voice was icy. 'We have to be at the airport in 30 minutes, so you two need to get yourselves together. Bring an overnight bag for this trip, the weather may close in. The car will be leaving in five minutes.' Then he turned and walked away.

Derrick followed Jake, without looking back, smoothing down his hair and tucking his shirt neatly into his trousers as he went. CJ staggered back against the door frame, rubbing the wetness of Derrick's lips from her own with the back of her hand, as hard as she could. A sob escaped from her. She couldn't believe what had happened. Derrick had assaulted her and completely set her up in front of Jake, but why?

He'd said Jake was still in love with his late wife and if that was true, why bother to make it seem like they were a couple? What message was he sending to Jake and why?

'The man's a snake,' she stormed, trying to stem the tears that threatened to flow.

Conscious she was now running late, CJ raced to the bathroom and swilled some mouthwash around to get the taste of Derrick out of her mouth. It was all she could do not to retch into the sink as she thought of it. Then she grabbed a few clothes and stuffed them into a bag, before picking up her coat and hurrying to the meeting point, feeling shocked and violated.

CHAPTER 23

'CJ, sit next to me,' Xanthe said, moving her bright orange rucksack to make room. She patted the seat invitingly and CJ was thankful there was one person happy to see her. Xanthe sat between her and Derrick, Jake in the front. Neither man acknowledged her.

'Finally, we're all here.' Jake's sarcasm was spoken through gritted teeth.

CJ shot a fierce look to the back of his head. He had no idea what she'd been through and hadn't even bothered to hear her side of the story.

The atmosphere in the car was tense but Xanthe didn't seem to notice, instead filling the silence with chatter. Derrick looked out of the window with a smirk on his face. How CJ would love to wipe that look off.

'Daddy, why are we all going?' Xanthe asked. 'Why don't we wait at the hotel until you've finished?'

'There's a storm coming,' her father said flatly. 'We should be fine to get back but if this business lunch takes longer and the weather closes in, then I want you under the same roof as me.

We have some rooms at the hotel on St Martin's at our disposal, just in case. You can do your lessons and have your lunch there.'

'Oh. We're not coming to lunch with you then?' The disappointment was evident in Xanthe's voice. After yesterday's day of fun, she was no doubt hoping for a repeat performance.

'No, but I've said to the hotel you can choose whatever you like from the menu.'

'OK.'

It was small consolation for Xanthe and CJ felt for her. But any sway she might have had was long gone.

Within minutes they were at the airport and had boarded the private helicopter, the sound of it shrouding the silence.

Jake stared resolutely at the view, his jaw set hard, barely paying lip service to the things his daughter was pointing out.

CJ was still trying to figure out what had gone on. Xanthe's tutor had no interest in her romantically, that much she did know. So what game was he playing? Was it some sort of misplaced loyalty to Jake's late wife, trying to ensure no-one ever took her place? That might be a part of it, but Derrick also gave the sense of someone out for himself. She realised her hands were balled into fists, as she tried to keep her rage under control. There was no way Derrick was going to get away with what he'd done, but first she had to think.

The flight was short and they were met on St Martin's by a member of staff from the hotel in a Land Rover, which whisked them the short distance to their destination.

What a far cry from the last time they'd visited, for the wedding of Tara and Sam. That time they'd arrived for a truly happy event; today the atmosphere was as heavy as the approaching storm.

In the hotel lobby Jake gave Xanthe a big hug. 'I'll see you later sweetheart. Work hard. Do you want to watch a movie this afternoon after I've finished?'

'Yes please. Can I choose?'

'Of course. Whatever you like. Within reason.'

'And can CJ watch it with us too?'

'Oh, she's too busy this afternoon,' Jake replied quickly, without bothering to look at CJ. 'We can't expect to take up all of her time. She has a business to run.'

Xanthe's face fell but she didn't protest and instead allowed herself to be led away by Derrick to start on her school work.

CJ was mortified. She would've loved to watch a movie with the two of them but Jake obviously didn't want anything more to do with her. She was in despair. It was one thing wanting space between them because of the feelings he still held for his late wife, but at least she'd hoped they could be friends. Now devious Derrick appeared to have scuppered even that, but for what purpose?

Jake ushered her through the doors in silence, avoiding eye contact.

'Look, about earlier,' she started.

'Save it, you don't owe me an explanation. You're both adults,' he snapped marching ahead to the private restaurant, CJ trailing in his wake.

Once again, the fresh local produce had been used to good effect by the chefs and the food was delicious, yet CJ merely picked at it. The only redeeming feature was that she was placed next to Douglas and Barbara. It was also their first visit to the Isles of Scilly and they regaled her with descriptions of their visit to the beautiful botanical gardens on the nearby island of Tresco. They told her about it in so much detail that CJ almost felt she had been there herself. It was a welcome distraction, particularly as Jake focussed on the couple to his right and pointedly ignored CJ, except when politeness dictated otherwise.

'You look pale today,' said Barbara, reaching across to pat her hand. 'And you've been very quiet. Hardly touched your food.'

'Hasn't been able to get a word in edgeways with us droning on,' interrupted Douglas fondly.

'True, but even so I sense something's not quite right.' Barbara nodded silently towards Jake who seemed engrossed in conversation. 'A falling out perhaps?'

CJ was mortified to feel tears forming and she tried to steel herself. Jake wouldn't approve of her making a spectacle of herself at an important business event. 'It was a misunderstanding, something that looked like something it wasn't,' she said quietly. 'Though I've not been able to explain, because he won't listen.'

Barbara patted her hand again. 'Then make him,' she said firmly. 'Douglas and I have been married for nearly 40 years and part of that success is never to let a misunderstanding fester.'

'Oh, we've not long known each other, we're not in a relationship, or anything like that,' CJ protested, stunned that the older, graceful woman could think otherwise. She just hoped Jake really was in deep conversation and couldn't hear what was being said; he'd be none too pleased.

'So Jake said.' Barbara gave her a knowing look. 'But whatever he says, I can see a young couple deeply in love from a mile off. Don't you think, Douglas?'

'Heck, I'm no expert Barbara, you know that. But you've never been wrong before. So, CJ, I guess she's hit the nail on the head.' The older man smiled kindly at CJ. 'Look, it never did any good to hold onto bad feelings. Jake's a decent man, he'll listen, I'm sure.'

CJ felt a bit brighter. Barbara and Douglas were right, she needed to clear the air. One way or another, she would make Jake hear the truth. Even though he was still ignoring her, she felt brighter as she tackled her smooth loganberry mousse and took in her surroundings.

Their private dining room was all in white and was simple and elegant. They were seated around an oval table which gave an air of intimacy despite there being more than 30 guests. To the right-hand side was a large chaise longue, its pink cushions adding a dash of colour. On the wide mantelpiece above the large fireplace, large vases burst with daffodils, their fresh scent permeating the room. All of this was dominated by the large floor-to-ceiling window, which ran along the whole length of the suite, with a view of the sea beyond.

CJ could already see the difference in the weather. The blue skies they'd enjoyed on their journey over had been pushed aside by a blanket of threatening grey. The sea was different too, the azure waters replaced by white horses topping waves, which frothed up the beach as they ran home.

'I think we should be heading back, Barbara,' said Douglas, before coffee was served. 'We have to get to London tonight and we'll be stranded here if we don't make a move.'

The pair stood up and Jake and CJ did too, to say their goodbyes. Many of the other guests also took the opportunity to leave, huddled into their coats as they headed swiftly towards private boats and helicopters.

As the couple turned to go, to CJ's astonishment, Barbara pulled her into an embrace and whispered into her ear. 'Good luck and remember, don't let the sun go down on an argument. Speak to him, make him listen.'

CJ nodded. Barbara was right. Whatever else happened, she was determined Jake would hear her out and she'd get to the bottom of what Derrick was up to.

CHAPTER 24

Jake was talking to some of the few remaining guests and so CJ took a moment to stretch her legs, stepping outside onto the terrace.

The wind had picked up and she could see the darkness of the rain-bearing clouds gathering on the horizon. If Jake wanted them to get back to St Mary's it would have to be soon. CJ didn't mind, both islands were bewitching and she'd welcome the chance to explore St Martin's once the storm had passed. If not, well she'd already planned to bring her mum and grandpa back here. Wherever she ended up today, the most important thing was to find time with Jake to explain. Then she remembered that vile Derrick was also here, and shuddered.

The thought of Derrick's lips pressed against hers, made CJ feel physically sick. She doubled over in the garden and retched into a flowerbed.

'Something wrong with lunch?' A smooth voice came from behind her.

'Jake.' She spun around and stood up all at the same time and staggered forward.

He caught her effortlessly, steadying her, and she saw see a flash of concern cross his handsome face but moments later it was gone, changed as quickly as the weather.

'It wasn't the food; it was something else. Something I need to talk to you about,' she implored.

He raised an eyebrow quizzically.

'It was about what you thought you saw this morning.'

'Oh that. Look, I'm not interested, CJ. What you get up to in your spare time is your own business.' He started to head back inside.

'Jake, wait!' she cried to his retreating back.

Ignoring her, he carried on.

Anger rose inside her. How dare he walk away and not give her the chance to put her side of the story? Especially after all she'd done for him this week. She marched after him through the reception area and into an empty lounge. Catching up with him she took hold of his shoulder and spun him around.

'What?'

'I need a couple of minutes of your time,' she said firmly.

'Look, CJ, how many times do I have to say it? I'm really not interested. In fact, it's more than that – I don't want to hear it.'

'Well unlucky,' CJ snapped, clenching her fists. 'I never wanted to come here and made that crystal clear. But you had other ideas, so I had to. Since arriving I've done everything you asked of me, gone to all your business meetings and acted like the dutiful Plus 1. I've put my life on hold for a week for you. And you've not behaved well in return, so the least you can do is listen to me for two minutes.'

Jake looked stunned and had the good grace to look bashful; he obviously wasn't used to being addressed in this way. 'OK,' he said grudgingly. 'Two minutes.'

He gestured towards a chair but she shook her head. 'Fine,' he said. 'But I could use a drink for this. You?'

CJ nodded and Jake left the room briefly, returning with two thick cut glasses. He passed one to CJ and she sipped it tentatively. The whisky burned its way down her throat, warming her insides. It made her feel a bit better.

'So, two minutes.' Jake glanced at his Rolex. 'Go on.'

CJ started to pace, something she always did when she was stressed. Jake leant against the mantelpiece, nursing his drink.

'I was doing my make-up ready for us to go, when there was a knock at the door. It was twelve-twenty so I was surprised because you're usually bang on time, not ten minutes early.' She looked at him earnestly and he nodded. 'When I opened the door, it was Derrick. I'd not seen him since he met us on the beach yesterday and didn't know he knew which was my room. Before I could ask what he wanted, he'd barged his way in and then tried to warn me off you…not that we're well…you know. I think he thought we were a couple.'

Jake raised a sardonic eyebrow, which CJ chose to ignore. If only he wasn't so damned handsome, leaning against the cool stone in his beautifully cut dark suit, which merely served to accentuate his incredible form.

Concentrate, CJ, concentrate.

This was not the time to lose track of what she was saying.

'Derrick told me I shouldn't get involved with you, that you were trouble. He also implied there was some sort of financial arrangement between you and me.'

'There is,' said Jake levelly.

'Yes, but you know financial in return for certain… well, favours.' CJ could feel her cheeks warming. It was so embarrassing and made her loathe Derrick even more.

'I see.' Jake's voice was calm but there was a steeliness about it too. 'Well Derrick knows damn well I would never pay for sex. And from what I overheard of the conversation, you made it clear you weren't interested in me. He was probably trying to find out what the deal was, no doubt to make a move himself. So, I don't think we have anything more to discuss.'

Jake slugged back the remaining whisky, slammed his glass down and made for the door. The first of the rain had arrived, driven forward by the increasing wind and it splattered against the windows.

'Hey, I'm not finished yet, wait up!' CJ followed Jake. She reached him as he made to open the door and grabbed his shoulder again, pulling him round to face her. 'What I want you to know is that we weren't kissing. Or anything else come to that.'

'It sure looked like it to me.'

'Jake, listen, he forced himself on me. Shoved me up against the wall and tried to kiss me. And I don't understand why, but I think it was because he knew you would see it.'

There was a long silence and once again CJ felt sick at the thought of Derrick's abuse. Like most women she'd endured her fair share of creeps over the years and found the best way to deal with it was to bury it deep and try to forget it. Having to say out loud what Derrick had done made her feel unwell. Her head started swimming and she dropped the glass, its brown contents spilling onto the carpet. The edges of the room seemed to decrease and all she could see was Jake's face, surrounded by darkness.

'Hey whoa, whoa, I've got you.' He caught her as she fell and carried her to the nearest chair. 'Here, sit. Put your head between your knees.'

CJ did as she was told, pushing her face into the comforting warmth of her woollen dress. The blood was thumping in her head. She could hear Jake moving around and the clink of a glass. Next, he was crouching down beside her, his gorgeous brown eyes full of concern.

'Sip this.' His voice was gentle and he held out some water to her.

She lifted her head and took a couple of sips. After a minute or two she felt a little better and gingerly started to sit up.

Jake took hold of her arm and gently guided her. 'Easy now, go slowly, don't rush it. You've had a shock.'

'I'm fine. I feel a bit better. Sorry.'

'Don't apologise,' he said, standing up and reaching across for another chair. He placed it in front of hers and sat down. 'It's hardly surprising, given what happened to you.'

'You believe me?' She looked up in astonishment.

'I do. Not least because I found you retching outside and now you've almost passed out. Plus, there's one thing I can say about you CJ Connors – you're not afraid to tell me it like it is.

So, if there was something going on with someone else, you'd have no qualms about letting me know.'

She smiled and the tension in his face eased.

'You're right about that, I'm not worried about speaking my mind to you.'

'You don't seem the type to lead men on, either.'

CJ was horrified. 'No. Why would anyone do that?'

Jake shrugged. 'People aren't always what they seem.' His voice was thick, as if speaking from somewhere dark in his soul. 'I'm so sorry that I didn't give you a chance to explain earlier. It must've been an awful experience for you and I should've listened.'

He searched her face and she nodded. 'I get it was a shock for you too. Derrick had obviously planned it to make it look like something it wasn't. But I don't understand why. I mean, I don't think he was actually interested in me. It wasn't like he was flirting or attempting to ask me out because no-one would go about it that way. If anything, he went out of his way to insult me.'

She looked off towards the churning sea, deep in thought. 'It sounds ridiculous but I think it was for your benefit. He messed up his hair so it looked ruffled and his shirt was already all over the place. Then he goaded me into saying what I did. I was trying to get rid of him, so said what I thought he wanted to hear to achieve that and of course it was right by the open door. The door he'd left ajar when he first came in…'

CJ faltered. To say the words meant reliving the memory of Derrick pressed against her, and she'd only just stopped feeling faint.

Jake stood and walked across the room. His body was tense, his strong shoulders drawn high. After a few moments he turned to her, face stricken. 'I'm sorry this happened to you CJ, truly.' His voice was hoarse. 'Because you're right. Derrick's actions were definitely for my benefit.'

CHAPTER 25

The storm was starting to pick up and there was no doubt they would have to stay on St Martin's for the night but Jake no longer noticed. Instead, his mind was in a different place and a different time. He went to speak and then stopped. He was about to talk of things he'd never uttered to another soul before. Could he trust CJ after knowing her for just a few days? Of course, he could take legal action if she broke his confidence, but by then the damage would be done – to Xanthe.

He glanced across at CJ now. She was looking at him earnestly, her hands folded in her lap. She was a good soul, he felt sure of it. It was a calculated risk but one he was prepared to take with her. Besides, after all she'd been through this week because of him, he owed her.

He gathered himself. 'Derrick is doing this because…'

No that wasn't fair. If he was going to do this, he had to tell the whole story, which meant going back further into the past.

He started again. 'You may know that Xanthe's mother died, more than three years ago.'

His voice was quiet and CJ leant forward to hear him above the rain. She nodded.

'What I'm about to tell you must remain between us, contained within these four walls.'

'Of course.'

Jake dug deep into his soul to find the right words. He had tried hard to push that part of his life away and now, having to face it, he wasn't sure he could make it.

'I loved her.' The words were finally wrenched from his throat and hung heavy in the room between them. Was he mistaken, or did a look of disappointment cross CJ's face? If so, it was gone now.

'I'm sure you did. Derrick said how extraordinary she was.'

Jake frowned. So that was what Derrick had been up to — trying to make CJ think he was forever off limits? The thought made him plough on quickly with his story. 'At least I thought I loved Melissa, but in the years before her death things changed. To be honest, I didn't even like her by the end. I've wrestled with the guilt of that ever since the accident.'

Jake had expected CJ to be surprised by this, after all the media coverage of his marriage inferred everything had been perfect. Yet she didn't seem to react at all, which was a first. He pushed the thought aside. 'I met her when we were very young. Eighteen, fresh out of school. I'd left England and was starting at the same drama school in the US. Into this whole new world came Melissa. She was dazzling and was always surrounded by adoring fans, male and female. All the women wanted to be her and all the men wanted to be with her. To my astonishment, she chose me.'

Even though he'd been snapped up as a model and later as leading man in box office-breaking films, Jake had never considered himself anything special. The fact Melissa had chosen him had always bewildered him. At that young age, he'd been unsure of himself and flattered by her attention.

'We married when we were 20, too young really. Our families weren't keen but that made us more determined and when we were in Las Vegas for my work one time – well, it seemed the right thing to do.'

Jake winced at the memory of his parents' reaction. And what did CJ make of it? He watched her impassive face. She was a professional psychologist, someone who'd made a living from making sensible decisions about relationships, albeit other people's. 'Please believe me when I say we married for all the right reasons,' he implored. 'We planned to stay together forever, at least that was my intention. And we did ok at first. Her father was a successful businessman and once he'd accepted me as his son-in-law, he took me under his wing. I learnt a lot from him – still do. I was fortunate, things went well for me and for her too.'

'I've no doubt you did it for all the right reasons, Jake.' CJ came to stand by his side.

As she did so, he got a waft of her scent, its light sweetness intoxicating. Desire punched him squarely in the guts and it took all his strength to carry on. But he realised he had to explain everything, if he was to have a hope of a future with her.

'Money was a big part of the problem.' He focussed on the story. 'Melissa had been brought up in a world of great wealth. Don't get me wrong, her parents are lovely and they hadn't spoiled her as such, but when you live that way, it's what you're used to. Everything is at a whole other level from the day you're born. Melissa liked the idea of starting from scratch with me, but wasn't so keen on the reality.'

It was something that troubled him about Xanthe. His own parents weren't poor but nor were they wealthy, so his childhood had been like most other kids'. Even though he encouraged Xanthe to work hard in her studies and to do chores for treats and rewards, the very nature of living in huge homes with staff, jet-setting around the world with him and all the other things they did because he was wealthy, were sure to have an impact. It was another thing he had to worry about, as a single dad. But he'd think about that another time.

'To me, the money we first made was an absolute fortune, but it was a pittance to her. On top of that I was working all hours to build my career, seizing every opportunity that came my way. Although Melissa worked hard too, she had a better view of work-life balance. I had no time to give her attention or do the things most people in their early twenties do. Not surprisingly, she started going out alone. She found me very boring, very quickly.'

'I doubt that was the case.'

Jake made a face. 'Then we had Xanthe. To me she was – is – perfect as you know.' His heart swelled as he spoke of her. 'I was lucky, I could do the job I loved and then come home to play with my daughter. It was the best of both worlds. But Melissa found her social life cut in half and her career on hold. While she loved Xanthe, she found the adjustment difficult. I was oblivious. Sexist really – on the rare occasions I did think about it I assumed motherhood was fulfilling enough and didn't realise that Melissa might want more.'

It was the first time Jake had admitted this out loud and it didn't feel good. 'Not surprisingly, things went downhill between us. We were too young to know how to fix it, too different and for sure, way too headstrong. It was grim for both of us.'

He stared across the restless sea, his mind casting back to the raised voices, the tears, the slammed doors.

'Is that why?'

CJ's words brought him back to the present and he turned to look into her lovely face. Why what?'

'Why you had an affair, Jake? Why you cheated on your wife?'

CHAPTER 26

CJ had expected Jake to react in a range of ways — denial, guilt, remorse. She'd seen it all before with Angus. Or merely a plain admission. But instead Jake just stared at her.

'What are you talking about?'

'The affair you had, when you were married to Melissa.'

'My affair?' An astonished look crossed his face.

She didn't respond.

'Oh, and I suppose Derrick told you that?' Jake's voice started to rise. 'That'd be right. A snake, sticking the boot in.'

Jake clenched his fists and a pulse was throbbing in his neck. 'It's time he and I had it out, once and for all.' He started to make his way towards the door. CJ couldn't believe his reaction.

'No wait, you've misunderstood.' He didn't seem to hear her. She didn't have any desire to protect Derrick but if Jake confronted him in this mood, anything could happen. 'Jake wait!'

He was almost at the door and she was a few steps behind. It was as if a red mist had descended and he was oblivious to anything else. She needed to stop him, quickly. 'Jake, it wasn't Derrick who told me about your affair. It was Tara.'

It had the effect she wanted. Jake stopped dead in his tracks, then turned slowly around. 'Tara? Tara Hemsworth?'

'Yes Tara Hemsworth, Kerchavel, whatever name she goes by now.'

'Tara said I'd had an affair? But that can't be right, why would she say that? What could....?' Jake frowned and appeared to be deep in thought. At least he seemed to have forgotten any ideas of confronting Derrick.

He caught her arm. 'CJ this is important. What did Tara say to you?'

'That you had an affair and that's why you didn't fancy settling down.' CJ was beginning to wonder if she had dreamt her conversation with Tara.

'Those were the actual words she used?'

'Well, no I'm summarising, but that's basically it.'

Jake's eyes were boring into hers. 'Look, can you remember exactly what was said? Word for word? It's important.'

'I don't know...' CJ cast her mind back to the beautiful wedding. She pictured Jake and Sam, laughing together and Tara coming to talk to her. 'She obviously thought we were an item,' she said slowly, as the events unfurled in her memory. 'And she was pleased, said something about giving up on you.'

Jake made a pained face and CJ had to smile.

'What else did she say?'

CJ concentrated hard as the pieces of the conversation started to fall into place. 'You no longer seemed interested in settling down. I remember because it made me cross – thinking you were wasting my time and that of my clients. And then she said....'

'What? What did she say?' Jake was watching her, expectantly.

'She said something about…they should've realised that, what with the affair and everything.'

'That's exactly what Tara said: what with the affair and everything?'

'Yes, yes, that's how she said it.'

Jake nodded. 'Well don't you see, she didn't say who was having the affair.'

CJ was trying to catch up. 'No, but I thought, I mean we'd been talking about you, so I supposed...'

To her surprise Jake pulled her into a hug. 'Well given my behaviour that night and since I can see why you would think that of me, so I'm going to forget all about it. But believe me when I tell you Tara wasn't talking about me.'

'She wasn't?'

'No.' Jake brushed a piece of stray hair from her cheek. 'She wasn't talking about me because I wasn't the one having the affair. Or affairs in this case. It wasn't me, it was Melissa.'

CJ stared at him with surprise and a wave of guilt flooded through her. All this time she'd thought Tara had been talking about Jake and she'd never thought to question it. Was it because of her own memories of Angus cheating on her? Is that why she'd assumed it was him?

'You do believe me, don't you?' It was as if Jake was reading her thoughts. 'One of my many 'attributes' is to be an arrogant son of a gun, so I can assure you I'd have no issue with admitting to an affair, if I'd had one.'

She nodded. That much was true. Jake was different in every way to Angus, who had tried to plead innocence, even though she had caught him in the act.

'Believe me, things got so bad there were occasions when it crossed my mind,' Jake continued. 'If Xanthe hadn't taken up most of the little spare time I had, I might well have strayed.'

'So, what happened?'

He took her hand and led her back to the chairs. It felt so natural and made her heart flutter with hope. Could they find a way through this? That might depend on what he said next.

They sat beside each other.

Jake's voice seemed lighter now, as if the weight of years of secrets was beginning to lift. 'I knew Melissa was starting to have affairs, at least I suspected she was. I thought about getting a private detective to find out for sure, but I couldn't have stayed with her if I'd known for certain. Which would have meant a broken home for Xanthe, meaning I wouldn't have seen her every day. Does that sound dumb?'

He looked at CJ earnestly, as if seeking her reassurance.

She shook her head. 'Not at all. You put Xanthe first and thought you could carry on and I can understand why. Though affairs aren't easy to ignore. I get the feeling things weren't quite as straightforward in the end?'

'No.' He made a face. 'I should have realised it would get worse. Even the cloud of suspicion destroyed our relationship. I couldn't go near her, thinking she might have been with others. The early flings, if I'm right about them, were light-hearted, flirtatious. I think it made her feel younger, brought her back to those days before we were married, when every face in the room turned to her.'

He sighed.

CJ remembered the photos of Melissa. She'd been beautiful, with her raven hair and striking blue eyes.

Her thoughts were broken by the sound of the door creaking. They looked at each other. Was someone listening to their conversation?

Jake pressed a finger to his lips, then crept silently across the room, the thick pile carpet deadening his footsteps. When he reached the door he flung it open. CJ watched as he looked up and down the corridor.

'No-one there. Must have been the wind. The storm's well and truly arrived. We'll definitely be staying here tonight.'

'There are worse places.' CJ gave him a soft smile.

For all the emotion and misery of the story he was sharing, CJ was relieved he felt able to confide in her. It meant he trusted her and she felt both honoured and relieved. Perhaps they could salvage something from this emotional week, after all.

'Xanthe will be finishing her lessons soon,' Jake added and CJ shuddered at the thought of coming face to face with Derrick. It didn't go unnoticed.

'Before then, there's something else you need to know.'

Her jaw dropped. There was more?

'My wife was having a few indiscretions and of course it wasn't good – god knows, not really sustainable, but at that point, things bumped along. I was tied up with my films and then building the businesses, and Xanthe took up all of my attention when I was home. Which I'm ashamed to admit, wasn't as much as it should've been.'

Something Jake was still in the habit of doing. Though hopefully this week might lead to a change? CJ certainly hoped so.

'Part of the reason – no, the whole reason I overlooked the affairs, didn't rock the boat was because I didn't want to lose Xanthe. I knew my regular absence would mean Melissa would likely get main custody and I'd be left seeing my daughter every other weekend, or worse. I wanted more.'

'So what changed?' CJ asked softly.

'Melissa. Melissa changed.' He looked down at his hands. 'She was obviously seeing someone else, that much I was sure of.'

When he looked up, his face was full of agony. 'This time it was different, because this time, she was in love.'

CHAPTER 27

'Who? Who was Melissa in love with?'

CJ felt devastated for Jake. It must have been the most terrible of times. Bad enough to know the woman you had committed yourself to was unfaithful and that your family life was at risk, but to realise she was in love with someone else…

'How did you find out?'

'You know, I didn't specifically.' Jake gave an ironic laugh. 'But there was something about her that changed. She was singing around the house, taking more of an interest in her clothes and appearance. I suppose you could say I recognised what she was like when we were first seeing each other, when we were in love.

'This time I did hire a private detective because I needed to be sure and I was scared, CJ.' Jake looked at CJ imploringly. 'Scared that this was the moment which would split our family apart. I was also still working through my own feelings for Melissa. Although I felt angry and betrayed, I'd been so in love with her – or at least the person I thought she was – it was hard to switch off my feelings completely.'

CJ nodded. She'd had her share of heartbreak in the past, but nothing as complex and difficult as the situation Jake had faced.

'As you can imagine, relations between Melissa and me had deteriorated over the whole time this had been going on.' Jake grimaced. 'We were barely civil to each other and she despised me. I thought she might make things difficult for me if we got divorced. Might go for sole custody. And while she wasn't always keen on the restrictions of being a mum, she did adore Xanthe. Plus, I had no grounds for saying Xanthe couldn't stay with her, because even if her mother wasn't there, we had staff…'

He trailed off, realising what he'd said. Great as staff might be, they were no substitute for parents.

'She's growing up fast,' CJ said softly. 'There's still time, but don't leave it any longer.'

'I know,' he said, studying her. 'I realise that now and have you to thank for it. Whatever it was I agreed to pay you is nowhere near enough. What you've taught me is priceless.'

CJ thought briefly of her own relationship with her father. She'd often wondered what her life would have been like if her parents hadn't divorced. They saw each other a few times a year and got on well but he'd recently remarried and was wrapped up in the lives of his stepchildren. At times CJ felt they were receiving the love and attention she and her brother should have had.

'Xanthe's lovely and for some reason thinks you're great.'

'Yeah, well she's always had strange taste,' Jake joked and they both laughed. 'Though you realise you've missed out there, Miss Connors?'

'How so?'

'You could've increased your bill and got away with it.'

'Well, there's still time. I've not invoiced you yet.'

It was a relief for both of them to lighten the mood for a few moments. As hard as the conversation was, Jake seemed happier. CJ wondered if it was because he'd been holding onto these feelings for so long, with no-one to confide in.

Even though it was the afternoon, the storm clouds made it look almost like night. The sea matched the sky in greyness, the white tops of the waves cresting as the swell began to build. CJ was glad of the comfort and warmth of the hotel. She thought she might get her book later and order some tea, before settling down in one of the plush sofas that were scattered around for the guests to use.

But first she intended to give Jake as much time as he needed to tell his story.

The door opened and a member of staff came in. 'Can I get you any refreshments?' the woman asked.

CJ noticed how she only glanced briefly in her direction but spent most of the time looking at Jake. He had that effect on people.

'Would you like something?' Jake asked her.

'A coffee?'

'OK two white Americanos please, a jug of water and maybe some biscuits? Also, my apologies – I dropped my glass earlier.' He nodded towards the brown stain of whisky on the light-coloured carpet.

'Not a problem sir, we'll soon sort that out.' The woman beamed at him and, collecting their empty glasses, withdrew from the room.

Satisfied they were alone, Jake turned to CJ. 'Are you feeling OK now?'

She nodded. 'I am. And thank you, you needn't have taken the blame for my spilling the whisky.'

'Not a problem. It was the least I could do after refusing to listen to you. And speaking of listening, are you OK hearing me talk about this?'

'It's fine. A problem shared and all that. I get the impression you've not spoken about this before.'

Jake nodded and walked across the room to lean against the large, marble fireplace. 'Where had I got to?'

'You said you'd tried to find out this time whether your wife was actually having an affair.' CJ found she couldn't say Melissa's name and she wasn't sure why. It was almost as if this was a part of Jake's life in which she had no place.

'You probably don't approve of my using a private detective. Nor do I really, though I still think it was necessary. I made sure I used the best in the business, someone who would be discreet. You met him actually, at the wedding. Tom Reynolds?'

CJ met quite a few people at Tara and Sam's wedding but she remembered Tom because he was warm and friendly and he and Jake seemed close. She remembered his broad, welcoming smile, so the last thing CJ would've thought was that he was a private investigator. Though until now she'd never given any thought to what a P.I. should look like.

'It's not something I took lightly, in effect spying on my wife. And it's not something I'd ever wish to do again.'

CJ was struck by this. To all intents and purposes, Jake didn't seem at all interested in starting a new relationship and after the story he'd just been sharing, she could fully understand why. But was his last sentence a hint that he might, after all, consider marriage again?

'I knew Tom would be discreet and quick and I was right,' he continued. 'I had the report in my hands within a week and it confirmed my worst fears.'

CJ sat upright. 'What did he find out?' she whispered. 'Did Tom discover she was having an affair?'

Jake's face was unreadable. 'Oh, he certainly did. He came back with times, dates, places, even photos of my wife and her lover together. I don't know if they'd tried to hide it – if they had, they'd not done a very good job. But either way, the information Tom discovered showed that Melissa was most definitely having an affair and appeared to be madly in love. And I was shocked to discover who it was.'

'Who was it?' CJ implored, leaping up from her chair. 'Who was the man Melissa had fallen in love with?'

CHAPTER 28

'Derrick,' Jake said flatly. 'Melissa was conducting an affair right under my nose with our daughter's tutor.'

CJ stared at Jake in shock, then jumped out of her skin as the door slammed shut again. This time they ignored it.

'Are you sure?' CJ asked. 'You're absolutely certain it was Derrick?'

Jake nodded, his mouth set in a grim line. 'Yep. No doubt about it.'

Even though the news came as a shock, the more CJ thought about it, the less she was surprised. Derrick was certainly a creep. Now she could understand why Jake was so angry when he came across what he'd mistakenly thought was the two of them together. 'But why do you still employ Derrick as Xanthe's tutor, especially after Melissa died? How could you bear him being around?'

'I can't, to be truthful,' said Jake. 'Every time he turns up there's an atmosphere. But when Melissa died Xanthe was obviously totally distraught. She clung, literally and metaphorically to those closest to her. One of those people was Derrick. And he did nothing to discourage it, as you might imagine.'

CJ made a face. She could certainly imagine Derrick taking advantage of the situation.

'I couldn't bear for Xanthe to go through those feelings of loss a second time by firing Derrick, much as I wanted to.' Jake rubbed the mantelpiece with his thumb, absentmindedly. 'I thought maybe I could get rid of him after six months, then after a year. And then it didn't happen. He knew I'd love to get shot of him and so he did his best to cultivate his relationship with Xanthe. So we three fell into an uneasy routine.'

CJ was about to ask more when the door re-opened and their refreshments were brought in.

'Would you like me to serve your coffee?' the waitress asked, setting the tray down.

'No, it's fine, we can manage. Thanks.' Jake pressed a note into her hand.

'Thank you.' She seemed astonished by his generosity and left sporting a big smile.

In silence, Jake poured the coffee. Then he lifted the plate of tempting biscuits and offered them to CJ, along with a side plate. 'I think you should have a couple of these. It will help, after your shock today.'

CJ nodded, and chose lemon shortbread. It melted in her mouth, the burst of citrus refreshing. She sank back and let the feeling wash over her.

'Better?'

She looked up to see Jake watching her. 'Much.'

He nodded and handed her a cup of coffee. 'This has changed things, you know. The incident this morning. Derrick won't get away with what he did to you.'

'I don't want to make things difficult...'

Jake put up a hand to silence her. 'Don't even think about it, CJ. It's not making things difficult. He assaulted you – and worse – it was to get at me. It's a crime.'

'His word against mine though. He'll say I led him on. People like that always do.'

'Well, it won't stop us trying. I think we'll make it stick.'

CJ's heart lifted a little — us?

Jake was already continuing. 'The least I can do is fire him. I can't trust him with Xanthe, that much is clear. I don't know what he might be filling her head with. It's something I should've thought about before.'

He looked stricken. 'Firing Derrick was my first thought when I got Tom's report. Melissa tried to deny it at first but the evidence was clear. When she realised she was busted, she turned nasty. Told me she'd make sure I'd see little of Xanthe.' Jake shuddered. 'That was my worst fear. I dropped my plan to sack Derrick, figuring I could do it later, and tried to reach a truce. In reality, all that achieved was to give both of us time to consult our lawyers.'

'Can I ask what happened on the day of the accident?' CJ stood and walked across to him, placing a gentle hand on his arm.

He smiled and her heart swelled. Then he looked away, seemingly to summon up the courage to continue. 'I was at home that afternoon and she tried to get me to discuss things but I refused. We'd arranged a formal meeting with our lawyers for the following week and I told her she'd have to wait. I was tired and fed up and thought it would just turn into a slanging match. But refusing to discuss it didn't go down well.'

He paused and looked out of the window at the grey sea. But CJ knew his mind was thousands of miles away, at his family home.

'Melissa stormed off to the stables, took her horse and galloped off. It was what she always did when she was furious, or happy. Whenever she felt very high — or very low — she'd go for a long, fast ride. Had done ever since she was a kid.' Jake's voice was strained, tense. 'Walt, our old stable hand suggested she wait until later. Not because she was angry, he'd known her a long time – but because he could see storm clouds gathering, lightning in the distance.'

No thunder and lightning today but the wind and rain still pounded the coast as the weather front rolled in from the Atlantic. The coincidence made CJ shudder.

'Melissa ignored Walt's advice of course,' said Jake. 'She was headstrong, knew her own mind — I liked that about her, especially in the beginning, but it did mean she would take risks. Anyway, the storm arrived and then her horse returned to its stable, without her.'

Jake moved away from CJ and paced the plush carpet as he was transported back to the horrors of that day. 'We started searching and it wasn't too long before she was found, lying on the ground…it was obvious she was dead. There was a tree which had been hit by lightning nearby. Everyone said the bolt must've spooked her horse and she'd been thrown and killed, but I've always wondered if it was because she was angry with me and was riding too fast…'

His words petered out and he looked at CJ with desperation in his eyes. 'Maybe if I'd listened to her, agreed to talk things through, she wouldn't have gone for a ride in the first place. Then she'd still be here. I feel terrible, CJ – what I did, what I said…I robbed Xanthe of her mother!'

The last sentence was torn from his throat and he collapsed into the nearest chair, head in hands.

CJ raced across and knelt before him. 'It wasn't your fault,' she said firmly. 'You were right not to engage with her, you had to think of Xanthe's future, for all your sakes. It was her decision to ride off, against the advice of Walt. And whatever speed she was going, lightning striking a tree would make even the calmest horse bolt. All of those factors led to her death, none of which were your doing.'

'I could have talked to her when she asked to though.' His voice was muffled against his hands.

'And the outcome would've been the same. You weren't getting on and so if you'd talked, it would've turned into a row and she would've stormed off in any case. Whichever way, she was going to be riding in a rage.'

She saw his body slump, as if a physical weight had been lifted from his shoulders. Presumably he'd stored this up for more than three years, ever since he'd found his wife's body. What a dreadful thing to have gone through.

He lifted his head and looked at her, his face wet with tears. It was as if he were searching her soul, to ensure she was telling the truth. 'I never looked at it that way. Just thought I'd robbed Xanthe of her mother, through my own selfishness.'

'Why do you think you were being selfish?' asked CJ firmly. 'You'd overlooked the affairs in order to keep your family together. I don't wish to speak ill of her because it's terrible for anyone to die so young, but she knew that by starting a relationship with Derrick it would lead to the end of your marriage and all the ensuing upset. She knew how much you loved Xanthe and so you weren't merely going to walk away.'

'No, never!' The words were wrenched from Jake as if they caused him actual physical pain.

CJ could hardly bear to see him in such agony. 'The situation was inevitably going to be fraught. It's horrible that she should've had such a terrible accident but it certainly wasn't your fault. Besides, no-one will ever know if she was riding fast when the lightning struck.'

Jake stared at her for a long time. Never mind the surging waves outside, she thought she might drown in his beautiful brown eyes, but it wasn't because she was falling for him that she'd reassured him. It was because it was true. Melissa's death was awful, a real tragedy, especially for Xanthe. But CJ didn't believe it was Jake's fault.

'I've never considered those things before, thank you,' he said at long last, his voice calmer. 'I don't think I'll ever completely shake off the feeling of 'what if' but you've made me see things more clearly. And you're right. If we'd tried to talk it would have turned into an argument and she still would've stormed off. We were both pretty forthright. And if that had happened, I might now feel even worse, if that's possible. But thanks to you, I can see it with some perspective.'

Jake leaned forward and brushed his lips against hers, gently, as softly as a summer breeze. 'You don't know what it means to me…'

His touch was too much for CJ and she closed her eyes, anticipating what it would be like to be devoured by his kiss. But then she felt him move away and looked up to find him staring at her intently. 'What is it?'

'I've been longing to kiss you since that moment in the garden, the first time we met.'

CJ's mind went back to their meeting. She remembered how he had leaned towards her, until they were millimetres apart, then whispered in her ear about making the most of the week. It seemed like a million years ago.

'You make it hard,' he said huskily, tracing his lips delicately across her jawline, causing a groan to escape her lips. 'Very difficult indeed.'

'Is that such a bad thing?' she murmured, her whole body on fire.

'Yes,' he whispered, stroking her hair.

'Why?'

'Because I vowed when Melissa died that there would only ever be one person I'd allow to get close to me again – Xanthe. The sole person I could trust. I swore never to let anyone else get close.'

CHAPTER 29

CJ let the words sink in for a moment, then pulled away sharply. 'So why get me to arrange dates for you, if you had no intention of being in a serious relationship again?' She stood and crossed her arms defensively. 'It may have meant nothing to you but all of those women are gorgeous and talented and have bought into the idea that they might be able to have a meaningful relationship with the people they're meeting up with. What was it to you – a game to see if you've still got what it takes? Chance for some easy sex with no strings attached?'

Jake looked stunned by her sudden outburst. 'Whoa, no, it wasn't like that and certainly not the sex part. Whatever you might think of me, CJ, I'm not the type of guy to string someone along in order to get them into bed.'

'So, what sort of game were you playing?' CJ demanded. 'I suppose I should be grateful that at least with me you were more honest, it was just another transaction.'

Jake splayed his hands out defensively. 'No, CJ, look you've got this all wrong. I've not explained myself properly.'

'Go on then,' she demanded, hands on hips.

He stood and took a step towards her but she stepped back, stopping him in his tracks.

'It's true that I felt that way when Melissa died and for a long time afterwards,' he said. 'But recently lots of my friends have been getting married, or are in long-term relationships. Melissa and I were ahead of most of them by getting married so young. Over the last few years my mates have been finding brilliant life partners who they can rely on and trust, so I briefly wondered if I should try again. That was why my team contacted you. At the time I had the best of intentions, CJ.'

He looked at her earnestly and she felt her body relax.

'Well, you met lots of great women, so what happened?'

'You're right,' he said. 'They were amazing and maybe I should've put a stop to it sooner because it wasn't fair, but I found I couldn't bring myself to take any of them out on a second date. I still had this fear deep down after my previous experience. It was almost as if these women were too brilliant.'

'Oh, big excuse, the women were too good for me,' said CJ tartly. 'I've heard all that before. It's such a cliché.'

'It does sound like an excuse, I know,' he said calmly. 'But honestly, it isn't. Look CJ, you know me well enough by now, I'd admit it if I'd been stringing you along. I could easily tie you up in legal knots if you ever tried to tell anyone I'd been less than honest.'

CJ glared at him but knew it was true.

'It wasn't that they scared or intimidated me. It was that Melissa was fantastic and dazzling too when I met her and I wasn't enough for her. I wondered if the same would be true of them; my gloss would soon wear off. And I know you can't tar everyone with the same brush, but it felt easier to back away. Though now, with you looking daggers at me, I'm wondering if that was my best policy.'

He grinned tentatively but CJ refused to smile back, though deep down she was glad he hadn't gone on a second date with any of her clients. Instead, she turned towards the floor-to-ceiling glass window. The rain was hammering against it and she traced a finger down one of the tracks it made. The raindrops reminded her of a tear and made her wonder how many had been shed by Jake and Xanthe in the dark days since Melissa's death.

'OK,' she said finally, turning around, to discover he was only a few steps away from her, watching her with a serious expression. Almost as if her opinion mattered.

'OK, what?'

'OK, I think I can understand where you were coming from.'

'Good. And for what it's worth I'm sorry. I never meant to lead anyone on.'

'I'm sure they're over you,' she tossed lightly and laughed at the shocked look on his face. 'As long as you don't do it again, I'm willing to keep you on my books.'

'Oh, don't worry, I wasn't planning on staying on your books.'

It was CJ's turn to look shocked. What did he mean? Was he giving up the dating game altogether? She could hardly bear the crush of disappointment.

'Why the sad face?' he asked. 'I thought you might be pleased.'

'Pleased? Why?'

Jake stepped forward and scooped her into his arms. 'Well, I know there's all that lost commission to consider but I plan to more than make it up to you.' He pulled her closer to him.

CJ's brain was scrambling to catch up. 'What do you mean? What are you saying? You want to date me?' she asked incredulously.

'Well, technically I already am.' A broad grin spread across his face. 'Though I'd like to take you out on a date where the only thing I'm paying for is dinner and not your time as well. If that would be acceptable?'

'Not sure I have much choice in the matter, given my current position,' she said, allowing herself to lean back into his arms.

'Is that a yes?'

'Yes, it's a yes.'

'Better seal the deal with a kiss though, right?'

CJ's breath caught in her throat as Jake's lips brushed against hers, gently at first as if he were still teasing her, before his need became more urgent. She could feel the fire pulsing through every part of her as his mouth devoured hers and heat flooded from his firm body, their passion and desire matched sinew by sinew.

'I've wanted to do this for so long,' he murmured eventually, nuzzling her neck. 'Was it obvious?'

CJ raised her eyebrows as she tried to focus on his words, whilst fighting the sensations stirring within her. 'No, it wasn't obvious at all,' she said. 'You deserve an Oscar for that performance. You gave me the impression it was merely a business arrangement and you had no intention of ever seeing me again once this week was up.'

'Hmmmnnnn, well I did think that at first.' He bestowed a series of small kisses along her jaw and then behind her ear. 'But I was intrigued and then you got under my skin.'

'Got under your skin, that's romantic,' she laughed.

'I don't want you to get too big-headed. Got to keep your feet on the ground.'

'And you're doing a great job,' she retorted, gesturing to her horizontal position.

As he laughed and moved forward to kiss her again, they heard a loud cough.

Quick as a flash, Jake took her hand and pulled her upright. Together they spun around.

CHAPTER 30

Derrick.

CJ shivered at the sight of him and could sense Jake's body stiffen beside her. Instinctively she placed a hand on his arm, to hold him back.

'Don't let me interrupt,' the tutor said slyly.

CJ was struggling to control her own anger and Jake's hands were balled into fists. How he could've borne being around the man who'd had a fling with his wife was beyond her.

'What do you want?' Jake's voice was a low growl.

'I thought Xanthe was in here.'

'No, she's with you having lessons.'

'We finished ages ago, had lunch and as there was still no sign of you, I said she could come down here and look for you,' Derrick said smoothly. 'She texted to say she'd found you in here but that you were busy.'

For the second time, CJ could feel Jake's body tense. 'When was this?'

'About 20 minutes ago. I texted back to say she should come back up but so far…' Derrick trailed off and he shrugged.

Twenty minutes ago? No one had come into the room since their coffee had been brought in. Xanthe certainly hadn't burst in looking for her father. And yet…

'The door banged,' CJ said urgently, tugging at Jake's sleeve.

He wrenched his gaze away from Derrick to look at her. 'What do you mean?'

'I mean when we were talking about…' CJ signalled with a nod towards Derrick. 'When we were talking about that, a few seconds later the door slammed. Made me jump.'

'But I checked the corridor, there was nobody there.'

'That was the first time, but it did it a second time, remember? I assumed it was the wind again. But what if it wasn't? What if it was Xanthe and she heard everything?'

Jake went pale. CJ could only imagine how stricken he must feel to realise his daughter might have heard what they'd been saying about her mother.

'We have to find her,' he said urgently and CJ nodded.

The pair raced from the room, pushing past a silent Derrick who merely stood and watched. No offer of help seemed to be forthcoming, even though a lot of the blame lay at his door. What a nasty piece of work.

'I'll look outside, can you stay here and ask the staff to search the hotel?' Jake said.

Fear coursed through CJ's veins. The storm was raging and she was afraid for both Xanthe and Jake if they were out in it. But she knew she couldn't stop a father from risking everything for his child and watched helplessly as Jake raced out into the tempest.

Hopefully Xanthe was still indoors and she could call him back. She hurried over to the receptionist who had watched Jake's departure with astonishment.

'Have you see Xanthe?' she asked quickly. 'Mr. Masterson's daughter?'

The receptionist shook her head and CJ asked her to contact the porters and other staff in the hotel. Within minutes all the staff were aware that the young girl was missing and were conducting a search of the building.

CJ had to do something while she waited, so she asked for the key to her room. Her overnight bag had been delivered and she quickly kicked off her court shoes and pulled the green woollen dress over her head, swapping them for jeans, a long-sleeved white T-shirt and her running trainers. Grabbing her raincoat, she headed back downstairs. The receptionist shook her head as CJ approached. No news yet.

One by one those searching inside the hotel returned, or called through to say they'd found nothing. CJ felt sick. For a child to be outside in this weather didn't bear thinking about.

Then one of the waiters from lunch burst in. 'I was just talking to Sharon, who's not on duty,' he told them. 'She's been reading in her room in the staff quarters and noticed a young girl heading across towards the back of the island. She banged on the window but the girl didn't hear. Says she called down to reception but it was engaged and when she looked again the kid was gone. She assumed that as the weather was so bad, she'd have headed back.'

'When was this?'

'Bit under half an hour.'

'It could be her; I'll call Jake. He went in the opposite direction.' CJ pressed the number on her phone and waited. After a few rings it went to answerphone. Frustrated, she rang off and tried again. Same outcome, but this time she left a message.

'Jake, it's me. It sounds like Xanthe went around the back of the hotel. I'm going to go and look for her.'

When she ended the call the receptionist spoke up. 'I don't think it's a good idea for you to go out in this on your own. I think we need to call the coastguard and you should wait for Mr Masterson.'

'I'll be fine,' CJ said. 'They can catch me up. I'll leave you his mobile number, if you can keep trying it for me?'

'Of course.' The receptionist passed CJ a notepad and pen and she quickly looked up Jake's number and wrote it down. She wondered, fleetingly, if she would ever know it off by heart but quickly pushed the thought to one side. There were more important things to be thinking about right now.

With the phone number safely in the hands of the receptionist, CJ put on her showerproof coat. She hadn't expected to need it for a full-blown Atlantic storm but it would provide a little protection. Then she headed towards the main hotel doors. As she was about to open them, she felt a hand on her arm.

Turning around, she did a double take; the man standing there looked so much like her own grandpa. He had the same wispy white hair, had once been tall but age had given him a slight stoop, though he stood up as straight as he could. He was wearing the uniform of the hotel.

'I'm so sorry, I'm in a desperate hurry,' CJ said gently. Had it been anyone else, she might have been more abrupt.

'Reckon you should take this, if you're minded to head out on your own. Though there's a high spring tide, so you're best to stay here,' he said, holding out a rucksack.

'What's in there?' CJ focussed on the bag and ignored his advice.

He nodded as if expecting as much. 'Emergency flares. Easy to operate. If you need help you let it go into the sky and we'll be able to see it from anywhere on the island and help'll come dreckly. There's a first aid kit in there too – though I hope you won't been needing it.'

'Thank you,' CJ smiled as she took it from him. 'I hope I won't need any of it either but I'm glad to have it.'

Then she slung the rucksack onto her back and opened the door. A blast of wind almost wrenched it from her hand.

'You sure?' the older man asked.

'She's out there all alone.'

He nodded again and watched as CJ ran out of the doors into the storm.

CHAPTER 31

Jake was trying not to let panic overtake him. Ever since Derrick had told him Xanthe wasn't with him and he realised she might have overheard his conversation with CJ, he'd felt sick with fear.

With luck, she'd have hidden in the hotel somewhere. She had her mother's courage and spirit which meant she might also have headed outside. If that was the case, well Jake needed to find her, and fast. Question was, which way would she have gone?

Logically, he'd turned left and ran along the road which cut through the island. It was dotted with cottages on both sides but their doors were firmly shut and there was no sign of anyone around. If Xanthe hadn't been missing, he too would've opted for an afternoon inside.

He was heading up the road towards Higher Town, one of the places where the boats landed with their cargo of tourists – not that any vessels were out at sea right now.

'Xanthe! Xanthe!' Jake's voice was starting to get hoarse. It was being cruelly whipped away on the wind too, so he found himself shouting louder and louder in the hope she could hear him. 'Sweetheart, where are you?'

Jake cursed himself for letting the situation reach this point. He'd wanted to get rid of Derrick when he'd first heard about the affair with Melissa but her threats had stopped him. Although it stuck in Jake's craw, Xanthe had suffered so much that he hadn't wanted to immediately rob her of her beloved tutor too, no matter what a turncoat he was. The months had gradually turned into years and they'd fallen into this way of life. Usually, Jake had no problem with taking tough decisions and he admonished himself for not doing so in this case. Even if Xanthe didn't hear the conversation, there was no way Derrick could stay on any longer and so she was going to be upset either way. All Jake had achieved was prolonging the agony for her.

First he had to find her.

Jake searched every track and pathway in turn, calling her name, shielding his eyes against the rain. He lifted a tarpaulin which was covering a boat, pulled up away from the water's edge. It would make a good place to shelter, or hide. Nothing. He peered into an old shed and rattled the door but it was locked.

Then he saw a missed call from CJ and was filled with hope that Xanthe had been found safe and well. Quickly, he looked for somewhere to shelter in order to be able to hear the message and protect his phone from the worst of the elements.

There was a low stone wall running along the side of the road and he ducked down on the other side. It wasn't great but it would have to do. He dialled up his messages. The sound of CJ's voice filled him with unexpected warmth. He was soaked to the skin, his suit jacket heavy under the weight of the rainwater, not that he noticed.

But his delight soon turned to dismay, when he heard the full message.

His blood ran cold. Not only was he searching for Xanthe on the wrong side of the island but it also seemed certain she was out in this tempest, and now so too was CJ. The two most important women in his life were in danger. He tried to call back but it went to answerphone:

'Hi this is CJ. I can't take your call right now but please leave me a message and I'll get back to you.'

Jake groaned with despair as he waited for the beep to leave a message. 'CJ.' The desperation was clear in his voice. 'Don't leave the hotel or you'll put yourself at risk. I'm going to head over to the other side of the island and if that was Xanthe I'll find her. Just stay where you are.'

Even if CJ could've heard his words right now, he already knew the feisty redhead would already be out there looking. Her compassion for others was one of the things he liked about her, but now it was putting her in danger. Trying to quell the fear which threatened to envelop him, Jake jumped back over the wall and ran back the way he had come.

***

The wind was so strong that it snatched CJ's breath away and she pulled her thin coat closer around her body.

A wide, grassy footpath led around the back of the hotel, past the large air conditioning units and the flats where the staff lived when they were off duty. The path squelched underfoot and CJ's trainers were soaked in a matter of seconds. It was slippery too but as a seasoned runner she was used to all sorts of challenging terrain. And soggy as they were, her trainers were far more use to her than the court shoes she'd worn to lunch. Thank goodness she'd thought to bring them.

The path ahead curved round to the right and for a moment was exposed to the full force of nature, the gale almost knocking her off her feet. CJ could see the waves crashing against the headland, throwing up white spray and foam. It was both frightening and magical at the same time.

'Xanthe! Xanthe!' she shouted, looking this way and that.

Where was she? And why didn't she turn back when she saw how bad the weather was? CJ's conclusion was that Xanthe had indeed heard the conversation regarding her mother and Derrick, and was so upset that even the wind and rain had failed to register. She continued along the path until she found shelter beneath a weather-beaten tree, whose limbs were bent and misshapen by a life facing the elements.

She tried to call Jake but realised she had no phone signal, even when she held it into the air. Maybe a text would get through? She started her message but the screen was getting so wet she feared it might pack up altogether. Given there was nothing yet to report, it would be better to keep the phone dry.

CJ tucked it into her coat pocket and set off again with renewed determination. The staff had told her the footpath turned and then wound its way back up the island, with pastures on one side and the rugged coast on the other, until it eventually met with the main road at Higher Town. The island was less than three miles long but in these conditions it may as well have been a thousand. And finding Xanthe was only half the battle. Afterwards Jake was going to have to spend some considerable time explaining things to his daughter.

Her own Mum's smiling face flashed into her mind. They were lucky to have such a close bond. It hadn't always been that way. Like many teenagers, CJ had clashed with her for a few years but it had all come good in the end, with the help of her grandpa as a calming influence. How hard it must be to lose your mother at such a young age. And now, Xanthe's memory of her was likely tarnished by what she'd overheard. Melissa's relationships with Derrick – or anyone else – had nothing to do with her love for her daughter and it would be awful if Xanthe thought less of her because of it.

CJ reached a split in the track. It was impossible to know which to choose. The right-hand turn seemed to head inland. If Xanthe had taken that route then she'd likely be wet and cold but otherwise OK, but if she'd gone the other way towards the exposed headland, well that could be a whole other story. It was a no brainer for CJ.

She'd not gone too far when she saw a flash of colour – bright fluorescent orange. CJ had seen it somewhere before but couldn't place where. It was today, wasn't it? In the car, then the helicopter…?

'Of course, Xanthe's orange rucksack!'

It was part way down one of the cliffs and by squinting, she could make out the figure of Xanthe. It was hard to see much through the driving rain but she seemed to be pressed against the hard rock face. What had happened? Was she OK?

'Hold on, I'm coming!' shouted CJ though her words were being tossed around by the wind.

She broke into a run, her trainers slipping and sliding on the muddy surface. Coupled with the uneven path, she had to slow up in places; if she were to sprain her ankle, or worse, then she'd be no use to anyone.

Stumbling on, CJ kept focused on the orange rucksack.

The tide was on the rise, which meant the large waves were creeping ever nearer to the ledge where Xanthe was perched, still clutching her bag. CJ's heart was in her mouth and it felt like an age before she'd reached the cliff top above, even though in reality it was just minutes.

'Xanthe!' she called at the top of her voice because getting the young girl to hear her could be a matter of life and death.

This time her words hit their target.

Xanthe looked up, her face soaked with a mix of rain and tears. 'CJ, help me!'

'It's OK I'm coming.' CJ slithered down the cliff face, trying to keep the fear from overtaking her, as stones gave way under her feet.

Using her hands to steady her, she winced with pain as the hard, jagged rockface grazed her skin but still she inched downwards, the spray from the wave tops splattering against her jeans and coat.

'Hurry, CJ. I'm scared.'

'I'm nearly there, hang on.'

A few short steps later and she'd reached the ledge. Xanthe threw herself into her arms and CJ had to put her hand out to steady herself. 'Whoa, whoa, careful now. Don't worry, I'm here.' She hugged Xanthe tightly, whilst looking tentatively over her shoulder at the crashing water a few feet beneath them.

Quickly, she drew apart. 'Now, let's get you out of here,' she said in a voice which sounded far calmer than she felt. 'But first let's see if we can get hold of your dad, let him know I've found you.'

'Will he be angry?' Xanthe's face was pale. 'I didn't mean to worry him, it's just I heard…I heard stuff and I ran and ran and ended up here.'

'No, he won't be angry, just relieved you're OK.'

'And is he OK? I don't want anything to happen to him.' Xanthe's face was stricken.

'I'm sure he's fine.' CJ could understand why, having lost one parent, a child would be so concerned about the welfare of the other. 'I expect he'll merely be keen to get out of this rain. Why, I'm as soaked as I was in the sea yesterday,' she said lightly, reaching into her coat pocket for her phone.

The signal was better here in this precarious position than when she'd been hurrying up the path and Jake answered immediately.

'CJ, where are you? Are you alright?'

His voice instantly made her feel better.

'I went back to the hotel to see if there was any news and they said you'd gone out searching too. It's great that you care but it's too rough out there, you should come back. I need to keep looking, there's still no sign of her and—'

'I've found her, Jake,' CJ burst out, trying to get a word in edgeways.

'You've what? I can hardly hear you.'

'I said I've found her, Jake,' she shouted. 'Xanthe. She's here with me.'

'She's with you and you're both safe? Where are you?'

'We're along—'

Beep, beep, beep.

CJ looked at her phone with dismay. The signal had dropped out again. She hadn't had a chance to tell Jake where they were but hopefully the staff in the hotel would give him the general idea. Even so, she tried to call him back but it was no good.

'Right then, Xanthe,' she said with more confidence than she felt. 'We need to get you back to the hotel. Are you OK to clamber up the way I came down? It's a bit of a scramble but I'll be right behind you.'

'I can't,' wailed Xanthe, biting her lip.

'Of course you can,' said CJ reassuringly. 'It might seem a long way but it isn't really. You'll do fine.'

'I can't because I've hurt my ankle. I was at the top of there.' Xanthe pointed to the top of the cliff. 'Then I slipped. I managed to grab hold of this scraggly old tree and it stopped my fall.' She nodded towards a weather-beaten bush, which had valiantly made its home in the middle of the rock face.

CJ felt a wave of nausea wash over her. Xanthe could so easily have fallen down to the rocks below and if the fall hadn't killed her, the crashing waves surely would have. But there was no time to think about that at the moment. For now, she needed to try to find a way to get them out of there alive.

CHAPTER 32

Whoosh!

The flare shot up into the sky, lighting it up with an orange-red glow.

CJ had never seen a flare go up before and she was amazed at how brightly it shone, even in the dark rain clouds. Seeing it cut through the gathering gloom gave her a sense of hope. She just prayed someone would see it—and soon.

They'd tried and failed to get back up to the top because Xanthe couldn't put any weight onto her injured ankle. It would've been tough in normal circumstances for CJ to carry her but the ground was steep and wet and they'd had to admit defeat. As the waves swirled ever nearer, she'd remembered the flares, reached into her backpack and pulled them out. In the driving rain she worked out what she had to do and then released it into the sky. Now all they could do was wait.

'Do you think someone will spot it?' Xanthe asked.

'Of course,' said CJ. 'They already know roughly where we are and this will help direct them to us more quickly.' She hoped what she said was true and that Jake or others were indeed nearby because she wasn't sure how much longer they could stay on the small ledge where they were perched. They were both shivering with cold and scared.

CJ closed her eyes and held Xanthe close. There was nothing more she could do until help came and she didn't want to watch the waves creeping nearer.

Maybe she was dreaming, because in no time at all she swore she could hear Jake's voice. She opened her eyes and strained to listen above the raging elements.

'Xanthe? CJ?'

There it was again and it was unmistakable.

'Jake!' she yelled back. 'Jake, we're over here!' She couldn't yet see him but jumped up and waved, whilst making sure they stayed balanced on the ledge.

Xanthe shouted too. 'Daddy, we're over here!'

In seconds Jake was above them. 'Are you hurt?' he called down.

'Xanthe's hurt her ankle, that's why we can't get back up to the top,' CJ called.

'Hang on, I'm coming down.'

'I don't think there's time.' CJ was watching a towering wave moving towards them at speed. Jake was fit and strong but he would struggle to reach them before it hit. She made a split decision. 'Wait there, I'm going to push Xanthe up towards you.'

She turned to the ten-year-old, whose face was pale and pinched and grabbed hold of her tightly, talking firmly to her. 'Right, Xanthe, we're going to get out of here. I'm going to help you up as far as I can and then you'll have to reach up and your dad will grab you, OK? You understand me? You have to reach up to him, as high as you can.'

The young girl nodded seriously and swallowed hard.

'Good girl. Let's go.'

CJ helped Xanthe up, then hurried her to the slippery cliff face that she'd slithered down earlier. Jake was part way down, making his way towards them. CJ glanced behind her and wished she hadn't. The wave was soaring towards them, cresting, like a giant predator.

She grabbed Xanthe around the waist and with a monumental effort, lifted and pushed her up the cliff in front of her as hard as she could.

'Jake, grab her!' she cried.

Xanthe stretched her arms out. Jake flew down to his daughter, grabbing her quickly before hauling her away to safety, just as the wave struck.

The water bore down on CJ and she was engulfed. It was like being tossed into a huge washing machine and her feet were pulled from under her. She held her breath and closed her eyes, her hands reaching and grabbing at everything they touched in turn as she was thrown around, but nothing seemed strong enough to prevent her from being sucked backwards towards the raging waters. She was completely at the mercy of the sea.

Then her right hand touched something and it didn't slip away from her but stayed firm. She twisted her fingers into it tightly and managed to reach her other hand across; it too caught hold. CJ hung on for dear life; her desperate fight for survival all-consuming. Finally, the wave slipped away.

CJ kicked with her feet to try to find something that would take her weight but there only seemed to be air between her and the rocks below.

Then she felt a hand grip hard around her left wrist and then the other.

'CJ, can you use your feet against the rock face to push yourself up? We have to get out of here!'

She looked up through the scrawny bush, which had saved her from being swept out to sea, into Jake's face. He was as white as a sheet, his jaw set firm. 'CJ, you have to kick. Ready? Let's go!'

She nodded and kicked as hard as she could, her feet touching the rock face and giving her just enough traction – coupled with Jake's pulling – to get her onto the ledge. Next he had his arm around her and was half pulling, half pushing her up the rocks towards safety.

'C'mon, CJ, c'mon we can do this,' he urged.

She had no doubt that another huge wave was bearing down on them but didn't waste time to look, not least because her legs might fail her if she did. With a Herculean effort she used her remaining strength to push herself up the face, grazing her hands and snagging the arm of her coat as she scrambled against the rock. Jake was beside her the whole way up. As they reached the top, CJ threw herself over, grabbing hold of Jake's suit jacket to ensure he came with her.

As they rolled onto the wet grass another wave crashed against the cliff, its spray soaking them. They both staggered away before falling back onto the ground in a heap of tangled limbs. For a few moments CJ was unable to move. She didn't care that the rucksack was digging into her back because the discomfort told her one thing –she was still alive. When Jake's handsome face appeared above her, his hair now dark from its soaking and his face etched with concern, CJ thought she could well have died and gone to heaven. But no, it appeared she was still here on earth.

'Are you OK? CJ, speak to me.'

'I'm fine.' She gave a weak smile.

'Are you hurt?'

'I don't think so, it's hard to tell…I've just gone ten rounds with a giant washing machine.'

'Don't even joke about it,' he said grimly.

Next Xanthe's face came into view. 'Are you alright?'

CJ gave her a reassuring smile. 'Don't worry, I'm OK.'

She started to sit up, helped by Jake. Then Xanthe flung her arms around both of them and they were pulled into a long bear hug, two blonde heads and one red, close together.

'I'm sorry,' Xanthe said. 'I'm sorry that I went off like I did. CJ, I didn't mean to put you in danger.'

She looked as if she might burst into tears but Jake pulled her to him and kissed the top of her head hard, as if he never wanted to let her go. 'Don't worry.' He had to raise his voice against the tempest. 'Did you overhear what we were talking about in the hotel?'

Xanthe nodded against him.

'Well, it's never a good idea to run off, you know that, don't you.'

Another nod.

'But I get why you did and I know you didn't mean to put people into harm's way. We'll talk things through together when we get back. And hey, we're all OK, aren't we?'

'Nothing that a dry set of clothes and a cup of tea won't cure.' CJ was trying to lift the mood. 'But can we please head back? I'm freezing now all the drama's over.'

'Oh, CJ, what's that on your coat?'

CJ twisted around to see where Xanthe was pointing and saw the red mark of blood. She checked herself and then realised it was coming from her left arm – she must've injured it when she was being swirled around by the water.

'Here, let me look,' Jake said, gently pulling up her coat sleeve and that of her T-shirt.

Along her forearm was a long, red gash.

'Is there anything else in the rucksack? A first aid kit or something?'

'I think so.'

Jake gently eased the rucksack from her, unzipped it and rummaged around inside. He pulled out a packet, tore it open with his teeth and then pressed the soft dressing gently, but firmly, onto the wound.

'Lift your arm up,' he instructed and CJ did as she was told.

She watched him tend to her. His lips were drawn together in concentration.

It'd be good to kiss him right now.

When he'd finished, she realised his face was pale and his jaw set hard.

'What is it?' she said, alarmed. 'The cut's not that bad, is it?'

'Oh, your arm will be fine. I was just thinking back to seeing you swept off the ledge by that wave…' He stopped as if the words were stuck in his throat, then finally whispered. 'It was one of the most frightening moments of my life. I don't want to go through that again.'

CJ thought how Jake had found his wife after she'd fallen from her horse. That was enough trauma for one lifetime and now he'd had to go through this nightmare today. 'Try to forget it,' she said soothingly. 'I'm fine. Xanthe's fine. We're all safe.'

His brown eyes searched hers for a moment and despite what they had been through, CJ felt on cloud nine. There was a depth to the emotion shown on his face, something that couldn't be faked, surely? If she wasn't much mistaken, she'd say his feelings for her were as strong as hers were for him.

Then Jake turned his attention to the dressing, peeling it back tentatively. 'OK, the bleeding seems to have stopped, it'll do 'til we get back. It's important to get out of these wet clothes, so let's go.'

Jake made a quick call to the hotel to call off the search party and to see if there was a doctor or nurse on the island. Then, together, the three of them made their way back the way they had come, Jake carrying his injured daughter and holding CJ's good hand. CJ had a big smile on her face the whole way, despite being sore, cold and soaked through.

As they approached the hotel, CJ glanced across the sea and could already see blue sky breaking on the horizon. The storm was about to blow itself out, allowing clearer skies to follow. Is that what would happen now for Jake's relationship with his daughter? Would the events of this week give him the release he needed to make a fresh start? And if so, might she be a part of a brighter future too? She hardly dared to hope.

CHAPTER 33

'Not broken, but a nasty sprain, which is why it was so painful. Let's get ice on it and elevate it tonight. She'll need to take it easy for a day or two and then she should feel better. If it doesn't improve, do see your doctor in a few days.' The nurse straightened up from examining Xanthe's ankle.

Relief flooded through Jake. 'Thank you,' he said earnestly to the woman, who lived nearby and had raced to the hotel in the vile weather, as soon as she heard a child had been injured.

CJ was resting against the door frame of Xanthe's hotel room. She moved to let the nurse pass.

'Now I need to look at that cut on your arm.'

'Oh no, it's just a scratch. I cleaned it off under the tap when I got back, it's fine.'

Jake wasn't having any of CJ's false modesty. 'I think you should look at it, if you don't mind, please,' he said to the nurse. 'She says it was nothing but she had quite a battering.' He shuddered as he thought of the close shave on the cliffs. When he'd first seen the flare light the sky, relief had flooded through him, but as soon as he saw how close Xanthe and CJ were to the waves, the fear he'd felt was indescribable. It had spurred him on and he'd crossed the distance between them in seconds, terrified he might be too late. Quickly, he tried to focus on what was happening now, instead.

CJ didn't protest but followed the nurse to her room. Jake turned his attention to Xanthe, whose foot was popped up on pillows. He needed to have a proper conversation with her, find out how much she had overheard and try to restore her loving memories of her mother. But she looked worn out, tucked up in bed. Instead, he switched on the TV for her and dropped a text to his mum, making sure his story was scant on details. Still, within seconds she was on the line.

'Hey, patient. Grandma wants to talk to you.' He held out the phone.

Xanthe brightened and within seconds was jabbering away to his mum, telling her all about the drama. Way too much detail too. He could only imagine what his mum was going to say to him later, once Xanthe was out of earshot. From the way she was describing it, it was a great adventure, rather than a near disaster. Hopefully she'd continue to see it that way. He'd call the family doctor in the morning and seek her advice about how he could best support Xanthe.

But while Xanthe was on the call, he wanted to check on CJ. Derrick seemed to have disappeared and so Jake had arranged for one of the porters to be stationed in the corridor between their two rooms just in case. He'd never thought of Derrick as dangerous before, but he was desperate and so they needed to be careful. Jake let the porter know that he was popping next door.

He was about to knock on CJ's door when it opened and the nurse stepped out. 'All done,' she said. 'She'd done a good job of cleaning it up but I've dressed it properly. It'll be fine.'

Jake thanked her and then went in to see CJ. 'Xanthe's on the phone to my mum,' he explained. 'They always chat forever, so I thought I'd come and see what the nurse said.'

CJ closed the door and they fell into each other's arms. She rested her head against Jake's chest.

'I'm sorry,' he whispered, stroking her hair.

'It's not your fault.' She spoke against him softly. 'Besides, the nurse thinks it's going to heal just fine.'

'That's good to hear.' He eased himself away, so that he could look at her properly. 'Why did you head off to look for Xanthe on your own? Why didn't you wait for me to come back?'

'I wasn't sure how far away you were,' she explained. 'When I heard that someone had seen her heading in the opposite direction to the way you'd gone, I thought I'd make a head start. I didn't really expect to find her where I did.'

Jake searched her face and she realised there were tears forming, He quickly looked away.

'What is it?' she asked, softly.

'You...you saved her.' His voice croaked as he spoke. 'Xanthe. If you hadn't found her when you did, then helped me to reach her on that cliff, I would have lost her.' The words were guttural, torn from his very soul.

He took her face between his hands and his eyes bored into hers. 'If I live a thousand years, I can never repay you for that. For saving the most precious person in my life.'

She pressed a finger to his lips. 'Don't think of it anymore. It's done. I was there and it worked out and that's all that matters.'

'But, I…'

'Really Jake. Anybody would've done the same.'

He snorted. 'That's not true and you know it.' Then he pressed his lips to the crown of her head. 'I feel terrible about the whole thing. Dragging you over here, because none of the dates led to anything, which as you pointed out was my fault. Then it leading to all of this, you injuring your arm and then nearly losing you too…'

The tremor returned to his voice and CJ hugged him tight, with her uninjured arm. 'I've actually loved it here, even though I wasn't too keen in the first instance,' she said. 'Meeting Xanthe has been incredible, she's so lovely. And the islands are beautiful – even in a storm. I could've done without the washing machine wave scenario but otherwise, it's been great.'

Jake felt his spirits lift. 'No mention of me on your list, though?'

'Oh yeah, I forgot about that. Meeting you was OK too. But I don't want you to get too big-headed.'

'Don't worry, where you're concerned I'm sure that's not going to happen. You've got my feet planted well and truly on the ground.' He took a strand of her auburn hair and tucked it gently behind her ear. 'Though it's a shame you forgot to include me, because you were starting to grow on me.'

'Grow on you?' she gasped. 'You make me sound like some sort of vegetable.'

'A very exotic vegetable. Not your common garden carrot, more one of those rare varieties which once tasted is never forgotten.'

'Cheek!' she said and went to give him a playful smack on the arm.

He was too quick for her and caught her round the waist, pulling her in close, his face inches from hers. 'I have something to ask,' he said cautiously. He suddenly felt unsure of himself.

'I'm listening.'

'After this week is over, would you consider seeing me again… soon? And Xanthe too, of course,' he added quickly, in the hope his daughter might seal the deal. He watched her closely and relief flooded through him when she nodded.

'I'd like that. I'll have to consult my diary of course but I expect I can squeeze you in.'

'Oh really?' he drawled lazily, still holding her close. 'That's good of you, I feel honoured.'

'So you should be,' she replied with mock haughtiness. 'As I mentioned before, I set up the dates, I'm not the date.'

'Oh yeah, I seem to remember something about that.' Before she could say any more, Jake lowered his face and his mouth enveloped hers, his tongue seeking hers. He felt the now familiar fire race through his body as she pressed herself against him. With her uninjured arm she stroked the back of his neck with her fingertips, and he groaned involuntarily.

'Jake,' she murmured in response and every part of his body ached for her.

If he didn't stop this now, things would go much further. He didn't want that. Not here, not now. When the right time came, he wanted for them to have all the time in the world to explore each other's bodies and enjoy every sensuous moment.

He stopped and drew himself away from her. A confused look crossed her face.

'Too tempting when we're alone in your room together.' He nodded towards the bed. 'Much as I could think of nothing better than taking you to try that out right now, I want to do this right. I want to see where this relationship goes, take it bit by bit – because I think we could have something special here. Do you?'

She nodded and he leant forward and kissed her briefly again before pulling back. 'My goodness you are beautiful,' he whispered. 'Inside and out. And believe me it's taking all of my willpower not to carry you over there right now.'

'Perhaps a cold shower would help? Or a walk in the rain? Maybe a nice cliff walk?'

'Funny…not. I think I've had enough cliffs and rain to last me a lifetime but to be fair, any kind of shower would be good right now.' Jake looked down at his suit trousers, which he'd been wearing since the morning. They were still damp and covered in mud. 'Tell you what, I'm going to go and freshen up.' He looked at his watch. 'Will you join us for dinner in a while?'

'Of course, I'd love to.'

'Great.' He went to leave, then turned. 'Just one thing. We're going to eat in Xanthe's room, and watch a movie. It's going to be the worst kind of junk food you can think of – you know pizza, fries, a bucket of ice cream. Is that OK?'

'My kind of dinner date.' She smiled happily and he darted back and gave her another long kiss.

Then before their feelings could overtake them, she pushed him away. 'Go on, go – see Xanthe.'

'I will but believe me, she'll still be on the phone to my mum.'

'Then go get your cold shower.'

He laughed and gave her a quick salute. Then he returned to his suite, with a big smile on his face and a lightness to his step.

CHAPTER 34

Jake had been gone from CJ's room for less than a minute when there was a knock.

'What've you forgotten?' she laughed.

To her horror it wasn't Jake who strode past into the room.

'Derrick!'

In all the drama of the afternoon CJ had barely given Xanthe's tutor a second thought. He hadn't joined the search party. Given he was still in the same clothes and they were bone dry and clean, he'd been lying low.

'What do you want?' CJ said. 'Given you did a good disappearing act when you were needed this afternoon, I'm surprised you dare show your face.'

Derrick didn't seem in anyway troubled by her words but went and sat in one of the armchairs. 'I need your help.'

CJ laughed. 'You need my help? You've got to be kidding? Why on earth would I help you?'

'Because you like Xanthe – and you're keen on her father too by all accounts,' he said, sporting an ugly smile. 'Don't try to deny it, it's written all over your face. I wonder, what was he up to in here with you for the past twenty minutes?'

He glanced across at the bed, no doubt putting two and two together and making nine.

'So what? We're both single and we're both adults,' CJ said defiantly, her arms crossed.

Derrick ignored her protestations and instead created a tent shape with his fingers and studied them intently.

CJ had a sudden idea and while he wasn't looking, carefully slipped her hand into her pocket. She pulled the item out a little way, tapped it a couple of times and slipped it back, before crossing her arms again.

'Of course you're an adult. You're also the owner of a business which is doing well.'

CJ swallowed. She had no idea where this was going but she didn't like the sound of it. What did her business have to do with any of this?

'I wonder what your clients would make of the fact you've been pursuing the handsome billionaire they'd previously been on dates with? He's a charmer, so I'm sure some of them were hopeful it would lead to more. Might have been set on it.'

That was it, the killer blow. CJ felt pretty sure her clients – most of whom were now friends – would understand perfectly. But if Derrick twisted the truth, as she had no doubt he was capable of doing, he could easily make her time with Jake seem sordid and in some way dishonest. Nowadays a few bad reviews on the internet could do serious damage.

'I didn't set out to fall for him,' she protested, knowing it would land on deaf ears. 'I came here to go with him to some business events, that was all. And you know that. You know there was nothing underhand about it.'

'Hmmmm, well I believe you of course,' Derrick said. 'But will everyone else? I mean it doesn't look great. No doubt you had lots of feedback from those who went on dates with him; who's to say you didn't use that information for your own ends, to ensure you met all his criteria.'

With that he looked towards the king-sized bed again, making CJ shudder.

'Of course, I'm all for supporting entrepreneurs, so it doesn't have to be this way.'

CJ didn't respond. She'd listen to what he had to say and then with luck, could get rid of him.

'Given you've invested so much time in Jake Masterson and no doubt know him pretty well, I thought you could use your influence to my advantage.' Derrick gave a faint smile. 'You see, I fell in love when I first joined the Mastersons. And before you jump to conclusions, I'm not talking about Melissa. She was great of course, but love? To be honest, I don't believe in it.'

CJ gasped. It was a wonder any woman could find this slimeball attractive.

Derrick ignored her. 'I fell in love with the wealth, the luxurious lifestyle. It was my first job as a tutor, I'd always worked in schools before. Some of those pupils were wealthy but there everyone is the same – wearing the same uniform, going to the same classes, in a pretty basic environment. This time I actually lived within it and it was intoxicating.'

He rubbed his hands together. 'I couldn't believe that people really lived that way and I wanted a piece of it, and not just as Xanthe's teacher. Melissa could see my potential and we would've made a great partnership. I didn't love her, but I was fond of her. If only she'd had more patience. But she was always feisty and wanted everything that minute, which unfortunately led to…well, it led to where we are now.'

He paused and seemed deep in thought for a moment or two, still studying his long fingers. Was this some sort of contrition? CJ felt sorry for Melissa. She'd obviously been taken in by him, while he'd seen her as a meal ticket, a way to make him wealthy beyond anything he could have achieved on his own.

If Derrick did feel some contrition, it was short-lived. 'She was on course to get a highly lucrative divorce settlement and we were planning to get married immediately afterwards. Melissa had been stupid enough to make it easy for Jake to find out about us and so I knew my position was precarious after her death. Thankfully Xanthe and I got along so well. I was her rock and poor Daddy couldn't bear to see her hurt again.'

Derrick laughed and it was all CJ could do to control her temper. She could fully understand Jake's actions now. Derrick would've made sure Xanthe couldn't do without him in order to secure his position. While Jake was grieving and feeling responsible for Melissa's accident, Derrick was like a snake, capturing his prey.

'I was there for Xanthe, comforting her and giving her support,' said Derrick, as if reading CJ's thoughts. 'With her relying on me, there was no way Jake was going to get rid of me. Xanthe would have been distraught to lose two people from her life in such a short space of time. He tolerated me and has done ever since. I knew things would change eventually, so wasn't totally surprised to find you together on the beach, with you flirting away.'

CJ's mind took her back to that happy day; first watching the incredible seals and then enjoying the calm waters of Porthcressa beach. Typical of Derrick to try to sully it.

He stood and walked towards her. 'Despite my efforts to make it look like we were getting it on, Jake seems rather taken with you and I can see why.'

CJ backed towards the open door.

Derrick didn't stop. 'Now that Xanthe knows about my fling with her mother, our relationship is blown. It means I'm forced to resort to the next best thing. Getting you to do my dirty work.'

'Dream on,' CJ retorted.

Quick as a flash Derrick grabbed her arm, twisting it painfully where she had injured it and using it to force her body against his. She gasped with pain, repulsed by the smell of his stale breath as he brought his face close to hers.

'Oh, I think you will,' he snarled. 'That precious company of yours that you've worked so hard for, with a question mark over how it's run? All I want is my fair share, a decent pay out. After all, I've invested years of my life into this family, one way or another. I need someone to make Jake see that.'

'You're sick!' CJ said, pulling her arm away sharply from his grasp.

'Maybe,' he hissed. 'But remember, I'm also all out of options. A desperate man and all that.'

'Leave her alone!'

Derrick and CJ spun around to see Xanthe, in her PJs and cream dressing gown, standing in the open doorway.

'Xanthe, I'm glad you're here. I wanted a chance to explain things to you.' Derrick's smooth change of tone even surprised CJ.

'It's all been explained to me, by my dad. I have nothing to say to you.' Xanthe's tone was steely and cold – beyond her years.

'Your father will have told you one side of the story but as I've always explained, you need to listen to every viewpoint before making a judgement.'

'I don't want to listen to you.'

Derrick put on what CJ guessed was his teacher-knows-best expression. 'Now come on, Xanthe, it's only fair. Besides it's what your mother would've wanted.'

CJ's sharp intake of breath caused both Xanthe and Derrick to look around. If Derrick's tutor-act had caused Xanthe to waver, she seemed to gain confidence in seeing CJ's horrified expression. How could he stoop so low as to bring her poor mother in to argue his case?

'You were playing tricks on my mum, just like you're threatening CJ.' Xanthe's voice was rising and echoing along the corridor. 'I used to like you but now I think you are the worst person I ever met. You ruined everything and I never want to see you again. Now, leave me, my dad and CJ alone!'

Derrick stood between the pair of them, like an animal stuck in a trap. CJ thought he might do something desperate, like grab Xanthe and take off with her, even though he couldn't get far. Just to be sure, she moved quickly to Xanthe's side. 'Go back to your room and get your dad,' she urged. 'As quickly as you can.'

Xanthe nodded and hobbled away, leaving Derrick glowering at CJ. He was inside the room and she was by the door and now the game was up, she knew he'd plan to make a run for it. She could slam it in his face, though that would only delay him by a second or two and would probably make him even more angry.

One thing was for sure, she didn't think she could stop him. Even though he didn't seem particularly fit, he was taller and bigger than her. Besides, she was tired from the exploits in the storm and her arm throbbed painfully.

As if reading her mind, Derrick said, 'Step aside, it'll be easier for you.'

'No way!' CJ felt she had to at least make a stand.

Derrick rushed past her, giving her a spiteful elbow to the ribs as he did so. Winded, she doubled over and watched him head towards the emergency staircase.

CHAPTER 35

'CJ, are you OK?'

The sound of Jake's voice was like nectar to her ears. In seconds he was beside her.

'It's OK…just winded,' she panted.

His face was pinched with rage as he guided her back into the room and sat her in the chair, which unbeknown to him, Derrick had vacated only moments before. His hair was still damp from the shower.

'Don't worry about me, he's getting away. He headed to the stairs.'

Jake searched her face as if checking that she really meant it.

'Go – but be careful,' she urged and quick as a flash he was off, sprinting along the corridor, through the doors and out of sight.

Immediately, CJ regretted her words. What if Derrick pulled a knife on Jake? She wouldn't put it past him, given his desperation. And after what had happened with Melissa, which led to Xanthe running off and being in danger, what would Jake do when he caught him? A chill ran through her. She had to stop him, so started running along the corridor in his wake. She made it down the three flights of stairs in record time, took a left turn and burst into reception.

'Oh, you got him!'

Derrick was standing there, looking forlorn, a hotel security guard on each side of him. A couple of other people were also hovering nearby, no doubt in case he made a run for it. Jake was leaning on the reception desk, explaining something to a member of staff. He turned when he heard CJ's voice, and hurried over.

'CJ, you should've stayed in your room. Are you sure you're alright?' Anxiety was etched across his face.

'I'm fine…but more to the point, are you? You didn't do something daft, like hit him did you?' CJ nodded in the direction of Derrick who was watching them intently and straining to hear what they were saying.

'Oh, I wanted to.' Jake gave a low guttural growl. 'I would have liked nothing more than to pummel him into a pulp – and believe me, that's something I've never felt before.'

'I'm glad you didn't because he would also like nothing better than for you to hit him, so that he could make a claim against you, or have you arrested. That's what all this has been about Jake. Melissa, his staying on as tutor and ingratiating himself with Xanthe; he wanted a big pay-off down the line.'

'What about Melissa? What did he say? And what do you mean, a pay-off?' Shock was written all over Jake's face.

CJ realised she'd have to choose her words carefully in case it sparked his fury again. 'I'll explain it all, but we need to go and see Xanthe first, check she's OK. But don't worry, I've got him Jake, I've got him.'

'Got me? Yeah right. I don't think you know who you're up against,' Derrick said from across the room.

Jake went to move, but CJ stopped him. 'Don't let him wind you up or make you as bad as he is. It's what he wants. Trust me on this…look.'

CJ fished around in her jeans pocket and held up her phone, triumphantly. 'When he wasn't paying attention I managed to record him,' she declared. 'Every word. His threats, his blackmail efforts, all of it.'

'You're bluffing,' said Derrick, though he'd gone pale.

CJ pressed play.

'You're also the owner of a business which is doing well…'

Derrick's words came out loud and clear for everyone to hear.

'It's all there,' CJ said. 'Enough for me to press for an assault charge, at least.'

'Assault? I never assaulted you.'

'That's not what the recording will say and I'm pretty sure there'll be some CCTV in both hotels to back me up too.'

Derrick gave a howl of rage and lunged towards CJ. Quick as a flash Jake stepped between them and as the tutor reached him, CJ could hardly bear to look. What would Jake do?

To her relief, he merely put his hand out to stop the other man in his tracks. Jake was by far the fitter and stronger man and Derrick stopped short. He must've realised he had no prospect of getting past him to reach CJ. In seconds Derrick was back in the custody of the security guards. Although he wrestled with them, the two men, assisted by their colleagues, overpowered him.

'The police say they'll be here as soon as the weather allows them to launch, which shouldn't be long,' the receptionist said hurriedly. She seemed anxious to get rid of this troublesome guest.

'Good, not a moment too soon.' Jake's tone was still low and dangerous. He turned to Derrick. 'Thanks to CJ, I can finally get you out of our lives. It's something I should've done years ago. So goodbye — until I see you in court.'

'Damn you, Jake Masterson. You haven't heard the last of me,' snarled Derrick.

'Oh, but I think I have. C'mon CJ,' Jake said, putting a hand out to her.

She took it without hesitation and realised that Jake was trembling. She looked up into his handsome face, and squeezed his hand reassuringly.

When they were safely in the lift, Jake sagged against its mirrored wall. 'Wow, didn't think that would get to me quite as much as it did,' he said, running his other hand through his blond hair, but still holding onto hers.

'It was bound to, there's so much unresolved stuff going on because of him. He was the embodiment of your marriage issues and instead of being able to move on and grieve properly, Derrick was always there as a constant reminder.'

'Is that the psychologist speaking?' Jake had a hint of amusement in his voice.

CJ shrugged. 'Nope, just a human being. I understand why you stuck him for so long…'

'That was for Xanthe's sake.'

'Of course, but ultimately it was extremely damaging for you.'

'I'd like to have damaged him,' Jake said. 'I hope you were impressed by my restraint back there, when he made a lunge towards you. It took all of my willpower to control myself.' He gave her a lopsided smile, which she returned. He was still holding her hand and she wanted to punch the air.

'I was impressed,' she laughed.

Then he took her face in his hands, before kissing her tenderly on the forehead.

'I'm so glad you're OK,' he said. 'And thank you. Thank you for everything you've done for me this week. My whole life has changed. Xanthe's too. I think...'

But whatever he thought was lost to her because the lift doors opened to reveal Xanthe, sitting on the porter's seat, while he stood by her side.

'Finally!' she cried. 'I was getting worried.' She hobbled forward to give Jake a hug.

'I told you to stay in your room with your foot raised.' He hoisted her up easily.

'I did, but you were gone ages.'

'Well, we're here now and we've got some important news for you.' Jake started heading back towards his suite with CJ walking alongside.

'You have?' An expectant smile spread across Xanthe's face.

'You bet. I spoke to the chef and he can make pepperoni, or ham and pineapple pizza...which do you prefer?'

'Can I have both?' Xanthe said tentatively and Jake roared with laughter.

'Cheeky! But as we've all had a rough day, I'll see what we can do.'

Jake gently placed Xanthe back onto her bed. He and CJ then plumped up the pillows behind her and under her leg, until she was comfortable.

'Grab a pew, CJ,' Jake said gesturing to the bed, while he tried to find a film.

Xanthe and CJ opted for a modern-day take on Sleeping Beauty. The pizza, fries and ice cream duly arrived and as CJ smelt them, her stomach gave a long deep rumble.

Later, she was completely wrapped up in the film when she realised Jake was trying to attract her attention. Xanthe had fallen asleep and he was signalling for her to join him in the other room. Carefully, they got up from the bed and tiptoed out, closing the door gently behind them.

'I was enjoying that film,' she said with mock indignation.

'Oh, do you need me to tell you what happens in the end?'

'Ha ha, funny.'

'I'm sorry, we can go back in if you like.' His tone was unusually flat. 'I've been thinking about Derrick. I never wanted anything to happen to Melissa but I'm so glad she never found out that he was using her. She would've been devastated. And Xanthe heard it?'

CJ nodded solemnly and Jake rubbed his chin; deep in thought. 'That's going to be quite a road we have to travel, Xanthe and me.'

'If there's anything I can do to help…'

His face softened. 'You've done enough already.'

She looked down at her hands. This was obviously something he wanted to do alone with his daughter. It was understandable but she still felt crushing disappointment.

Did Jake realise? Because he said gently, 'I could really use your advice though. I'm not great at this parenting lark, as you can tell.'

Her heart skipped a beat. 'Are you asking me in a professional capacity?' she grinned.

'Of course. But are you sure you wouldn't rather change careers and become a detective instead? Your idea to record Derrick was inspired.' His face was full of admiration. 'Genius. It means we've got him.'

'I hope so,' said CJ. 'I'd hate to think of him going after someone else like this. But he's a slippery character, I guess we can't take anything for granted.'

'Oh, believe me, I will do everything I can to ensure he doesn't do that sort of thing again to another family. My marriage was already in tatters so he can't be blamed for that, but he went on to do some serious damage. I have every intention of stopping him from doing it again, if I can.'

'Good.'

The air sparked between them. CJ wasn't sure who moved first, but next they were in each other's arms.

Jake held her tightly. 'When that wave hit…' he said, his voice ragged.

'Shhhh, forget it now, it's over.' She placed a finger gently against his lips.

Still holding her gaze, Jake kissed the tips of her fingers. The touch of his lips was almost imperceptible, yet CJ felt her whole body start to tremble. The tiny kisses on her skin felt like rivulets of fire. He took her hand in his and kissed the palm.

'CJ.' His voice was hoarse.

'Jake,' she moaned in response.

His other hand entangled in her hair and she felt his fingers gently pulling her towards him. CJ didn't resist, she couldn't even if she'd wanted to. She could hardly breathe, with the heat of his body flooding between them. His mouth found hers, gently at first, softly seeking, before she felt his need build and become more urgent, matching hers. Soon she was lost as the kiss deepened, devouring her, his earthy scent dizzying, threatening to overwhelm her. The drama of the day, the storm and Derrick all faded away as she was enveloped in Jake's caress, allowing her burning desire to meet his…

'Dad! CJ! You're missing the end.'

Whatever spell was being performed in Xanthe's film, she'd broken theirs. They pulled apart quickly, Jake immediately turning to his daughter and ushering her back to bed, seemingly able to change from the height of emotion to parenting mode, like the flick of a switch.

CJ watched his retreating back and put her fingertips to her lips, drinking in his lingering scent. Her heart was still pounding. Then she realised to her dismay that she was totally sunk. Tomorrow they'd be returning to St Mary's before the onward journey home. Normally, catching up with Mum, Grandpa and her friends filled her with pleasure, but not this time.

As she listened to the sound of Sleeping Beauty coming from Xanthe's room, CJ realised this was no fairy tale. In those stories everything came good and they all lived happily ever after. But she'd fallen head over heels in love with Jake Masterson, with no clue as to what the future might hold.

CHAPTER 36

Jake slept badly and woke early. He pulled back the heavy drapes to see the sun starting to climb the sky. It was hard to imagine that a fierce storm had blown across this enchanting island less than 24 hours ago. Realising he wasn't going to get any more sleep, he got up.

He tiptoed into Xanthe's room and listened to her soft, gentle breathing. Thank goodness she'd managed to rest after her ordeal. After CJ had gone back to her room, Jake had sat by Xanthe, long after she had fallen asleep. He'd wanted to sit there for the whole night, so shaken was he by nearly losing her. Eventually, exhausted, he forced himself to go to bed. The rooms were next door to each other after all. Despite feeling bone tired, sleep had come in fits and starts, punctuated by nightmares of waves, Xanthe's face, Melissa riding her horse and CJ tumbling away from him.

He needed to focus on now, put those dreams behind him. A run would help. He didn't want to leave Xanthe's side but knew he needed to get out and work off his pent-up adrenalin. The hotel staff were great, so he made a quick call to the concierge to make childcare arrangements in case Xanthe woke up. He threw on his gear, then when the lady member of staff arrived, he headed outside.

The difference in the weather could not be starker. Pounding his way along the lane, Jake enjoyed St Martin's simplicity and rustic charm. Daffodils grew wild in the hedges, the willows sported their catkins and the pretty cottages now looked warm and inviting. It had a different feel to St Mary's, but each island was stunning in its own way. Every few yards he saw tantalising glimpses of the sea, which had already returned to stunning hues of deep blues and aqua greens.

Jake made a vow to make a return visit to the islands, with time to explore properly. He realised it wasn't just Xanthe he pictured travelling with him, but CJ too. He couldn't imagine the Isles of Scilly without her there. Frowning he lost his stride, so stopped and leant against a five-bar gate, on the edge of a field carpeted in green velvet grass.

He took in the beautiful view; it really was paradise. But the truth was he was too preoccupied with thoughts of the future to make the most of the present. Jake had been through enough pain to last a lifetime — not least battling with the storm for Xanthe and CJ, a few short hours ago. He didn't want to be in such a vulnerable position again. He'd vowed throughout the week to make himself immune to CJ, but nearly losing her to the waves had almost torn him apart and showed how ineffective his efforts had been. Question was, what to do next? And what did she want?

Some cows chewing grass in the next field turned to ponder him for a moment before resuming their breakfast.

'You're no help with an answer,' he told them.

Exercise usually helped clear his mind and so he set off again, pushing his body to the limit as he ran the length of the island. Gradually, like the weather, his thoughts started to clear. A path forward began to form in his mind; so much so, that by the time he returned to the hotel he knew what he had to do.

***

Her last day on the islands. CJ didn't know how to feel. She and Jake had seemed so close last night but when she woke up, there was a text from him to say that Xanthe was still feeling sore and so they'd see her when they were ready to leave.

With no suggestion she should join them for breakfast, CJ made her way down to the restaurant alone. Even the stunning view over the now calm sea, did little to lift her spirits. Yesterday, she'd felt she and Jake were close to admitting their feelings for one another – now it would seem he was more distant than ever.

'How's the arm?' he asked casually as they met in the hotel lobby for the journey back to St Mary's.

'It's fine,' she lied.

In fact it had throbbed painfully all night, partly from the original injury but also from Derrick twisting it. CJ felt tired and stressed, failing to appreciate the lovely helicopter ride back to St Mary's. Jake spent most of the trip pointing out things to Xanthe.

An hour later and with all her bags packed, CJ stood in the garden of the hotel looking towards Samson for the last time. The clouds were drifting lazily across the sky, casting large shadows onto the waves. A gull cried overhead. Soon she would be back home, catching up with Lauren who was desperate to find out what had happened this week. In no time at all this trip would be a distant memory, a dream. She took a deep breath of salty sea air and closed her eyes.

'Thought I'd find you here.'

CJ jumped out of her skin. In front of her, on the other side of the picket fence was Jake. He gave her a cheeky wink.

'Will you stop startling people?' she admonished. 'And please move out of the way, you're ruining the view.' He was as easy on the eye as any landscape she could think of, not that she was going to let him know that.

Undaunted, he sprang over the fence to stand beside her. For a moment he too was silent, taking in the landscape.

'I thought you were packing?' said CJ.

'I confess I'm not good at that sort of thing. Xanthe on the other hand…'

'Xanthe? You've left your ten-year-old daughter to pack for you? With her bad ankle?' CJ's jaw dropped open.

'To be fair, she offered.' Jake tried to sound as casual as he could. Truth was, while he wanted to speak to CJ alone, it was tough wrenching himself away from Xanthe. 'Don't worry, it's all laid out on the bed so she's sitting down and I'm paying her. Oh, and Brooke is helping too. Don't look at me like that – Xanthe wanted to do it.' Jake splayed his hands, to emphasise his innocence.

'If you say so. Sounds like you're ripping her off.'

'If you knew what I was having to pay her, you'd say it was the other way around,' Jake said. 'Anyway, I had an important errand to run.'

'Oh really?'

'Very important.' His voice was softer now as he reached across to gently take her hands in his. CJ hardly dared move as Jake turned her to face him. Looking into his handsome face she felt her heart might break into pieces and, to her horror, she could feel tears pricking the back of her eyes.

Jake looked serious and seemed to be having trouble finding the right words. He never seemed short of things to say usually, so CJ began to worry. What was it he needed to talk to her about that was so difficult?

'CJ,' he said finally. 'You know I said I'd like us to go on a date when we leave here.'

She fluttered with fear. There was something in his tone she didn't like. 'Yes,' she said cautiously.

'Well, I've changed my mind.'

CHAPTER 37

A wave of misery engulfed CJ.

They'd got so close yesterday but that was because he'd confided his deepest secrets to her as a trusted friend, coupled with the near-death experience they'd all gone through. It was enough to make anyone emotional. Now Jake had seen things in the cold light of day and thought differently. The problem was, she loved him as much today as she had yesterday. What an idiot! She knew what Jake was like, always backing away from anything serious, and yet she still fell for him. He could have any woman on the planet, so why did she think she had a chance?'

'I see,' she said, trying to keep her voice from wobbling. She'd not give him the satisfaction of seeing how devastated she was. 'That's fine.'

'Fine? That's fine? Jake raised his eyebrows. 'Are you saying you're OK with not dating me?'

CJ shrugged. 'Whatever.'

'Whatever?'

'Hey, if you want to be short-sighted and miss your chance with me, well that's your loss.'

He laughed and drew her into his arms, much to her surprise. 'Short-sighted, eh? You're probably right. But if you'd let me finish, Miss Connors, I was going to say that I don't want to go on one date with you. I want to break with tradition and go on a second date too. Maybe even a third.'

CJ pushed herself out of his arms and stood with her head cocked to one side. 'You want to go on a second or third date? Are you sure? I mean you are the master of the one-date wonder. That's what you're starting to be known for.' Although she was going along with the joke, CJ's heart was soaring as high as the clouds above.

Jake wanted to see her again and again…

He shrugged. 'I realise I have my reputation to consider, but thought I'd make an exception. I was assuming you'd be willing to meet me more than once, though now I'm not so sure.'

'It's a big assumption and I'll have to check my diary…but I think I could agree to that.' CJ stepped forward, took Jake's face in her hands and kissed him gently on the lips. He responded immediately, his mouth seeking hers, softly at first, before the searing passion they shared, turned it into a deep kiss filled with longing and hope.

'I don't think our first few dates should be anywhere near a hotel room though,' he said huskily. 'I used up all my willpower in not hitting Derrick, not sure I've got much left to resist you.'

CJ felt the same. She wanted this man who possessed her soul, to possess her body too, but not quite yet. For now, she kissed him back, hard, meeting his need for her and demonstrating her own desires.

It was a long time before they pulled apart, CJ's eyes shining with happy tears. 'You know we have a helicopter waiting for us?'

'I know.' He groaned. 'Our timings have left a lot to be desired. And I'm going to have Xanthe on my case any moment.'

'Should we tell her? You know, that we're planning on seeing each other?'

He brushed her cheek softly with his fingertips. 'I think she's a step ahead of us to be honest. You remember what she said when we went on that day trip?'

CJ tried to remember but it wasn't easy with Jake stroking her face, sending shivers right through her. 'Something about… having someone in your life?'

'I was telling her about your dating agency and said you were trying to find someone for me and she said I already had someone. I think she could see what we couldn't.'

'Clever girl.'

'She gets that from me.' Jake thumbed his chest.

CJ gave him a playful shove. At the same time her phone beeped and she pulled it out of her pocket. There was a text from her grandpa but she couldn't make any sense of it.

Excited about the trip later – almost as good as seeing you. x

CJ reread it, a puzzled look on her face.

'Something wrong?'

She held the screen up to Jake. 'I don't understand what he's talking about. I hope he's OK?' She felt anxious. Why would Grandpa be talking about a trip? Was he getting confused? She looked into Jake's face anxiously, to find him sporting a huge grin.

'Damn, I was hoping it would be a surprise.' He took her hand and squeezed it reassuringly.

CJ frowned. What did Jake have to do with this?

'I hope you don't mind but when you said your grandpa loved helicopters and had never been in one before…well, I thought as we were flying you back home, it made sense to let him have a ride in mine when we get there. After all, I have put his precious granddaughter through the wringer this week.'

'You're not wrong.'

Jake made a face. 'I decided to surprise you, so I tracked down your brother and got in touch to arrange it. Your grandpa should be waiting for us with your mum. I hope you don't mind? I didn't mean to…'

CJ squealed with happiness and threw her arms around his neck. 'Fantastic, thank you so much. He's going to love it; I can't wait to see his face.'

Jake hugged her back. 'Don't get me wrong, I'm more than glad to do it for him, but I have to confess, it was you I was thinking of.'

She stepped back and looked into his handsome face.

He met her eyes. 'The thing is, CJ Connors, despite my best efforts, I seem to have fallen hook, line and sinker in love with you.'

CJ thought her heart might stop. Had she heard correctly, because it sounded like Jake had said he was in love with her? And yet, the look on his face told her it was true. 'That's good news, because despite my loathing you in the beginning, I've fallen in love with you too.'

This time, their kiss was long and slow, as they realised they had all the time in the world to be together, enjoy one another. A deep warmth and feeling of joy spread through CJ. She never wanted it to end.

Finally, Jake pulled away. 'Hey hang on a minute – you loathed me when we first met?'

'Yep, pretty much.'

He gave a low whistle. 'Wow. I hadn't realised I was starting from such a low base.'

'Pretty much as low as you could get.' CJ motioned to the ground. 'Down there.'

'So, when all's said and done, I've done a pretty amazing job.'

CJ laughed. How on earth was he spinning this?

'To have gone from that low.' He turned and pointed to the sky. 'To right up there. Pretty good turnaround in a matter of days.'

'Hey, who said you're up near the clouds?' CJ took a mock swipe at him.

'Oh I dunno, something in the way you kiss me.'

'Well, speaking of sky, we're running late. You're not going to make a great first impression on Grandpa if you keep him waiting.'

Jake glanced at his Bremont watch and grimaced. 'True. We'd better get going. Ready?'

CJ nodded and took one last look across to Samson. How her world had changed since she'd first seen the uninhabited island. Then she slipped her hand into Jake's and together they walked back towards the young girl who was about to become a big part of CJ's life.

Suddenly Jake let out a hoot of laughter.

'What's so funny?'

'You remember that first night at Sam and Tara's wedding?'

CJ's mind went back to the beautiful event. 'Of course.'

'And you were crying about something. You said it was because of the song that was playing, that it got to you here.' He thumped his chest.

'I remember,' CJ said cautiously. 'What are you driving at?'

'I said the lyrics were about an old woman and her husband who'd been together for years.'

'Yes. Emotional.'

'They're not.' Jake stopped walking and looked at her.

'Not what?'

'The words to the song, the lyrics. They're not about an elderly couple. They're about some bloke in love with a woman from afar.' He chuckled. 'I made it up to see why you were really crying and you fell for it. Just like you'd fallen for me. Your tears that night were for me.'

She rewarded him with a playful thump on the arm.

'Ow, what was that for?'

'For trying to trick me and for being big-headed,' CJ said tartly and she let go of his hand and walked on ahead, only to have him block her path.

'For the record, I can't remember the song and am absolutely certain that any tears were to do with the wedding and not you.' She pushed past him.

'Deny it if you like.' He darted from side to side. 'But you have to admit it was because of me.'

'I'm not admitting anything.' She tried to stifle a laugh. 'Now please get out of my way. I am an extremely busy and important person.'

'OK.' he gave a bow. 'Step forth, my lady, be on your way but remember – I know how you really feel…and I never forget.'

She laughed, then pretended to shove him as she passed. He exaggerated staggering backwards, before catching her up and taking her hand again. They were nearly at his suite now, ready to tell Xanthe that they were going to be seeing a lot more of each other. Hopefully she would be pleased. One thing CJ vowed to do was make sure Jake had the time and space to become a proper dad.

'There is one issue we need to resolve.' Jake interrupted her thoughts. He was rubbing his chin thoughtfully.

'Which is?'

'Payment,' he said. 'Now we're officially dating, technically I don't have to pay you for accompanying me this week, do I? Surely that's covered by the dating agency fees?'

'Nice try,' CJ said. 'Actually, I'm going to have to charge you double.'

'What for?'

'Danger money. I wasn't expecting things to be quite this dramatic.'

'Neither was I.' Jake squeezed her hand and grimaced.

'And with regards to the dating agency, well, I would hate word to get around that you aren't a man of your word – someone who doesn't pay his bills.' CJ turned and looked at him, a wry smile on her lips.

'You wouldn't?'

'It's a shame that your company hasn't kept its side of the bargain… Now, where have I heard those words before?'

'Unfair!' he said, with mock outrage.

'There's nothing unfair about it,' she said, as they reached the suite. 'I am a businesswoman with a hugely successful company, and a professional reputation to consider. If you look at your contract, you'll see I've more than kept my side of the bargain. Because, Jake Masterson, I've finally found you the love of your life.'

THE END

Thank *you* so much for buying *Hired Date on the Islands*,
I am so grateful that you chose it.
Reviews can make a big difference to authors, so if you can spare a few minutes, it would be fantastic if you could leave a review on Amazon, or other sites for book lovers.

Thank you!

Want to hear about future books
by Dove Devereaux?
Sign up to my newsletter at dovedevereaux.com

Dedicated to my own feisty, fun and fabulous redhead – my daughter Evelyn.
Thank you for the joy you bring me every day

ACKNOWLEDGEMENTS

Thank you for choosing Hired Date on the Islands and spending some of your precious time reading it. I hope you enjoyed finding out about CJ and Jake, as much as I enjoyed writing their story.

Huge thanks go to my Editor, Sara Naidine Cox. This is the first book we've worked on together and it was an inspirational journey. I am very grateful for her considerable expertise, support, good humour and enthusiasm. You can find her at www.saranaidinecox.com.

Trusted beta readers are a rare find and I want to express my gratitude to mine: Rosemary Cole (who read it twice), Sarah Evans, Justin Leigh and Tracey Smith. Also, to copy-editor Helen Baggott.

The Isles of Scilly Wildlife Trust is a fantastic organisation, kept busy looking after the wealth of flora and fauna on the islands. They shared their expertise about the seals with me and I was very glad to give them a little donation in return. If you want to find out more and/or make your own gift, you can visit their website at ios-wildlifetrust.org.uk.

The fantastic cover was designed by the talented Georgina Moore and you can find her at ghdesignexeter.co.uk. If you want to see the next book cover ahead of everyone else, sign up to my newsletter at dovedeveraux.com.

Last but not least, thank you to my lovely family for being so patient, encouraging and loving.

You can find out more about the beautiful Isles of Scilly on my website dovedevereaux.com.

HIRED DATE ON THE ISLANDS

By Dove Devereaux

First edition published April 2022
ISBN No: 978-1-9168722-3-3
Paperback Edition

For enquiries, contact the publisher at dovedevereaux.com

Printed in Great Britain
by Amazon